AN UNTIDY DEATH

Simon Brett

**SEVERN
HOUSE**

First world edition published in Great Britain and the USA in 2021
by Severn House, an imprint of Canongate Books Ltd,
14 High Street, Edinburgh EH1 1TE.

Trade paperback edition first published in Great Britain and the USA in 2022
by Severn House, an imprint of Canongate Books Ltd.

severnhouse.com

British Library Cataloguing-in-Publication Data
A CIP catalogue record for this title is available from the British Library.

ISBN-13: 978-1-78029-128-4 (cased)
ISBN-13: 978-1-78029-805-4 (trade paper)
ISBN-13: 978-1-4483-0543-8 (e-book)

All Severn House titles are printed on acid-free paper.

Typeset by Palimpsest Book Production Ltd.,
Falkirk, Stirlingshire, Scotland.
Printed and bound in Great Britain by
TJ Books Limited, Padstow, Cornwall.

To
Frankie Fyfield,
with love

ONE

'My mother's going to kill herself,' announced Alexandra Richards on Littlehampton Beach.

I was quite taken aback. I knew that Ingrid Richards had a problem – otherwise her daughter would not have been consulting me – but I didn't realize it was that serious.

'That is,' Alexandra went on, 'if I don't kill her first.'

This somehow made things better. Just standard-issue mother/daughter conflict . . .?

Perhaps I should explain the basics. My name's Ellen Curtis. I run a company called SpaceWoman. No, nothing to do with astronauts. My job description, printed on my cards, invoices and the Skoda Yeti which is my work vehicle, reads: 'Decluttering and Interior Restyling'. I help people when they've got too much stuff . . . or when the stuff they've got gets too much for them.

Alexandra Richards was a typical client. I don't know how she heard about my services, but she contacted me through the SpaceWoman website and asked to meet. Her mother lived alone in a situation of 'increasing chaos' and Alexandra was 'worried about the Health and Safety issues, apart from anything else.'

I don't have an office where clients can visit me. Very few have ever come to my home, only when it's been an emergency. I live in a three-bedroom house on the northern outskirts of Chichester, and I try to keep my personal and work lives separate. Though I can't compartmentalize my brain quite so easily – I'm always thinking about my clients – I do try to keep the house as my own space. My two grown-up children are, of course, always welcome there. My daughter Jools, busy working in London, rarely visits. But my son Ben, studying graphic design at Nottingham Trent University, often comes to Chichester during vacations or in times of need.

Normally, I'd visit a new client at their home, but Alexandra Richards lived in Hastings, way off my regular patch. That patch, incidentally, goes along the south coast from Portsmouth to Brighton and to the north as far as Petersfield or Horsham. So, Alexandra and I had to fix somewhere to meet. I first suggested her mother's flat, the scene of the crime, as it were, but she was adamantly against that. No surprise to me. In a lot of cases, the hoarder is totally unaware of the enquiries being made on their behalf – and would indeed be deeply affronted to know there were any such enquiries. One of the common qualities of hoarders is complete unawareness that they have any kind of problem.

Obviously, a lot of my work is highly confidential and over time I have compiled a list of suitable venues for private meetings. Depending on the season, I'll suggest a coffee shop one can sit outside or a pub. A busy pub is often an ideal place for an intimate discussion. Everyone's too preoccupied with themselves to consider eavesdropping.

If the weather's good, I prefer to suggest meeting outside. There are all kinds of quiet places in the Sussex countryside. Private places to sit and talk. Even better, private places to walk and talk. Best of all from my point of view, private places to walk and talk by the sea.

I had fixed to meet Alexandra Richards on the beach at Littlehampton. Just by the East Beach Café. That's a multi-award-winning building designed by Thomas Heatherwick, which looks like the rusty shell of some primeval mollusc. It's one of the town's proudest boasts, another attempt to smarten Littlehampton up. But the resort's ingrained tackiness has always resisted the march of gentrification. The Waitrose that opened there didn't last long.

There's a car park next to the café. Alexandra and I agreed that we'd discuss her problem as we walked along the front, then maybe have a coffee on our way back to the cars.

She looked somehow faded. I would have put her in her forties, maybe early fifties, getting on for my age. No wedding ring, and she made a point of telling me, almost as soon as we'd said hello, that she lived alone, she'd never been married and didn't have any children. She needed to get that one out of the way quickly.

The she gave me a short résumé of her life. She'd been a teacher, an experience which she gave the impression she hadn't enjoyed much. A legacy from her grandmother had enabled her to give that up and now she did some charity work. Unspecified charity work.

Tall, slightly lumpy, with a pale freckled face and biscuit-coloured hair that didn't quite qualify as auburn, Alexandra Richards wore the kind of clothes that had been chosen not to draw attention to herself which, perversely, made her look slightly eccentric. And drew attention to her. A beige raincoat, though it was a warm May day, and almost-masculine brogues.

The tide was low. The beach at Littlehampton slopes very gradually. High water reduces it to hillocks of uneven shingle, while low tide exposes acres of cement-coloured sand. Swimmers have to walk out a long way before the water reaches even their waists.

Had it been high tide we'd have walked along the promenade, bordered by a strange piece of artwork made up of wooden slats, some painted in bright colours and claimed to be the 'longest bench in the world'. But that time of day we could go on to the sand. I suggested to Alexandra that we walked to the right, towards the mouth of the River Arun.

Her appearance had made me suspect she might be shy, but she turned out to be very forthright. Almost dogmatic.

'It's got to a point,' she said, 'where I realize I have to do something about my mother.'

'How old is she?'

'About to be seventy-five.'

'Does she live with you?'

'God, no.' The thought actually made her shudder. 'She lives on her own.'

'How is she mentally?'

'All marbles in place. Or perhaps I should say that she's as sane as she's ever been.' The line was deliberately ambiguous.

'And your father?'

'I've never seen much of my father.'

'Ah.' There was a whole history there, but it wasn't the moment to investigate it. 'Where does your mother live?' I asked.

'Brighton. Well, "Hove actually", as everyone says.'

I knew the reference. When asked where they live, residents are reputed to say, 'Hove, actually', to distinguish them from their more raffish neighbour.

'A flat in Hove,' Alexandra went on. 'That's where she's ended up.'

'Implying that she has lived in a lot of different places?'

'You could say that. All over the bloody world.'

'Does that mean you had an unsettled childhood?'

'Why do you ask?' Alexandra demanded sharply.

'Something in your tone of voice,' I suggested.

'Huh. Look, this isn't about me. It's about my mother.'

'Of course,' I said, hiding my scepticism. In my line of work, I often learn as much about the person who draws attention to the problem as I do about the one who actually has the problem. Alexandra Richards seemed to fit neatly into that box.

'She's always collected paper,' Alexandra went on. 'Books, magazines, newspapers – particularly newspapers. She claims she has some filing system for them, but so far as I can see, they're just piled up randomly. And she chain-smokes.'

'Ah.'

'Gauloises. Those terrible French cigarettes that smell like tyres burning. Can't get them in England now. But, needless to say, Ingrid has an ex-lover in Paris who keeps her supplied.'

Interesting, that she referred to her mother by her first name. As I do with mine.

'And,' said Alexandra, with an air of resignation, 'she drinks.'

'I see. So, you're worried that . . .?'

'I'm worried that one night, halfway down a whisky bottle, she'll forget to stub out one of her Gauloises properly, pass out and . . .'

I nodded. She didn't need to spell it out. 'And you're consulting me about her safety in the flat?'

'Exactly that.'

'From what you say of her, it doesn't sound as if your mother would welcome my intrusion into her life.'

'You're right there. She'd hate it.'

I wasn't fazed by that. It wasn't unusual. 'Is she reclusive?'

'God, no. Rather the reverse. Gregarious to the point of depravity. Any excuse for a party – and if there is one she's always the centre of it.'

'She sounds like quite a character,' I said. It's a description I rarely use as a compliment.

'She's that all right,' said Alexandra in a resigned voice. 'When Ingrid walks into a room, she immediately monopolizes all of the oxygen.'

We stopped for a moment. There still weren't many people on the beach, dog-walkers, pensioners taking their daily ration of exercise.

'The thing is . . .' Alexandra continued, as if sharing a great confidence, 'and this makes everything somehow more complicated . . . my mother's quite famous. I don't know if you can imagine what it's like growing up with that . . .?'

'Oh,' I said. 'I think I can.'

'Are you sure you won't have another drink?' asked Fleur.

'No,' I said wearily. 'I've told you many times. I can't risk losing my licence. I need the car for my work.'

'Huh,' came the predictable response. 'I'm sure you could get work in places you could walk to. There must be an enormous demand for cleaners in Chichester.'

I didn't rise to it. I'd heard it too often. Why my mother constantly downgrades my career from decluttering to cleaning, I have no idea, but she'd been doing it so long that I no longer give her the angry response she so craves. She had always diminished me and played down my achievements. In most mother/daughter relationships, the analysis would be that the older woman was jealous of the younger, but in this case, there was nothing for her to be jealous of. She had a level of celebrity, I was just a working widow. And although she'd never take this on board, there was no area of her life in which I had any desire to be competitive.

In her time, Fleur Bonnier had been a moderately successful actress – no, sorry, her current taste for the politically correct would demand that I say 'actor'. And perhaps I'm being mean to put the 'moderately' in there. She was successful. There were a good few months of which she was the flavour. Perhaps, to be fair, years. She was still to be seen in ancient British movies screened at strange hours on television. Never playing the lead . . . the flighty friend, the earlier lover rejected in favour of the female star, the murderer's wife, that kind of part. But she did them well. Fleur Bonnier was a trouper.

Unfortunately, those months or years of her success had coincided with my childhood. Once her theatre friends had stopped praising her 'bravery' in having a child out of wedlock, Fleur rather lost interest in me. Evenings she was on stage, daytimes she was filming for movies or television. I got used to being farmed out to more or less unwilling relatives and friends. I got used to not letting it get to me.

As I got used to calling her 'Fleur'. Her idea, obviously. Initially, to give the totally false impression that we were girlie chums. Later, because a galumphing teenager who claimed her as a mother didn't do much for the age she was trying to live down to.

Fleur always blamed any shortcomings in her mothering skills on the demands of her profession. Though I don't think it would have made that much difference if I'd seen more of her, if she'd been a stay-at-home mum. Her consuming obsession with herself didn't leave any excess affection available for something like a daughter. She had always given me the impression that her life would be more convenient if I wasn't part of it. Apart from anything else, having a child did rather interfere with her complicated romantic entanglements.

I don't want to imply that Fleur and I were permanently at daggers drawn. I had long since lowered my expectations of what might be expected from her as a mother and learned not to respond to the permanent trickle of salt with which she dressed my wounds.

She was currently in one of the more settled periods of her life. Hardly acting at all – she'd had her moment in the sun – Fleur Bonnier was now married to a Chichester solicitor called Kenneth, who spent his weekdays in the office and his weekends playing golf. He gave her free run of his gold card and she suggested – often in public and embarrassingly – that he was rewarded by a sex life beyond his wildest imaginings. Like many of my mother's boasts, that was one I took with a whole cellarful of salt.

I had agreed to have Saturday lunch with her in the café at Goodwood Hotel and Health Spa, where her morning had been spent in variegated Lycra having a gentle gym workout. She calculated that this justified a boozy lunch. As ever, she wanted me to match her, Chardonnay glass for Chardonnay glass and, as ever, I had to remind her of the importance of keeping my driving licence. It was a conversational square dance whose steps we had shuffled through many times before.

'Have you heard from Jools recently?' Fleur asked.

'Not for ten days or so, no.'

'I had a call from her last night.' There was smugness in the statement. Fleur prided herself on her closeness to her granddaughter, with the implication that I wasn't as close to my daughter. Which was quite possibly true. Family tragedy had made Jools shut up like a clam. I couldn't get her to have a serious conversation with me. She was much happier engaging in shallow banter with her grandmother. Together, the pair of them giggled like schoolgirls, Fleur claiming empathy with the younger generation. And again, there was the implication that I was something of a sourpuss, not showing any interest in the world of disposable fashion which my daughter inhabited.

Though we'd never talked about the subject, Jools knew I disapproved. I'm afraid – though I don't know why I should apologize for it – that doing what I do has only strengthened my green principles. And I find it hard to forget the statistic that 300,000 tonnes of garments are burnt or buried in the UK every year. Most of it the kind of clothes that Jools prizes and writes about.

'She was telling me about an *influencer* she'd met,' Fleur went on. 'Do you know what an "influencer" is, Ellen?'

'Yes,' I said wearily. 'Influencers are people who have a large social media presence and are paid to endorse various products.'

'Yes.' Fleur's tone was a little miffed. She had looked

forward to enlightening my ignorance on the subject of influencers. 'I think it's only a matter of time before your Jools becomes an influencer herself, you know. She seems to have so many contacts in the fashion world.'

'I'm sure it's something she would love to be,' I said, trying not to sound snide. It was true. There was nothing Jools would like more than having a worshipping following of young women, following her fashion tips on social media.

'Hm.' Fleur looked at me beadily over the edge of her wine glass as she changed the subject. 'And how's Ben?'

'He's fine,' I said, ready for the usual insinuating criticism of my son.

'You hear from him more often than you hear from Jools, don't you?'

I shrugged. 'He keeps in touch. Texts mostly. Then the occasional long phone call. As I say, he's fine.'

'Good.' But, of course, Fleur wasn't going to leave it at that, was she? 'Still got the girlfriend, has he?'

'So far as I know, yes. Tracey. Seems to be working very well.'

'Good,' she said again, before moving into carping mode. 'And you still haven't met her?'

'No.'

'Seems strange, doesn't it? Not introducing his girlfriend to his mother?'

'I think that's up to Ben, isn't it?'

'Maybe. Still seems strange to me.'

In spite of myself, I was getting riled. The temptation to remind Fleur how few of her lovers she'd introduced to her daughter welled up in me. I was in my teens before she introduced my father (not an encounter that prompted any bonding instinct – or even interest – in me). But I resisted the urge to strike back at her.

Perhaps it got to me because there was an element of truth in the insinuation. I was disappointed by the fact that Ben hadn't suggested introducing Tracey to me. But stronger than that feeling was relief that my son was in a relationship that seemed to be working. He'd had a fairly chequered history with women. Never had any difficulty in attracting them. When he was on form, Ben was charismatic, he could charm the birds from the trees. But he wasn't good at sustaining relationships. They always started well, but ended in break-up, pain, and anguish.

In contrast to the distance between me and Jools, I had always been effortlessly close to Ben. He was easy to love. Just like his father. Sadly, he had inherited other, less benign, characteristics from his father. I know I'm sometimes overprotective of Ben, but I have my reasons for that.

'Seems strange to me,' Fleur repeated, 'that Ben doesn't want to introduce his girlfriend to his mother. Or his grandmother. This Tracey . . .' she mused, preparing to slide the knife in once again, '. . . do you think he's ashamed of her?'

I managed to finish the lunch without losing my temper. Fleur paid. She always paid. She was very generous with Kenneth's money.

My mobile had blipped while we were at the table, but I didn't check for messages until I was back in the Yeti in the car park. Only one. Voicemail.

A rather precise, slightly nervous voice.

'Hello. I hope I've got through to the right person. My name is Edward Finch and I have a problem of far too much clutter in my house. I'd be grateful if you could get back to me. My number is . . .'

The message suggested that Edward Finch was elderly, of the generation that still didn't quite believe mobile phones recorded the numbers of incoming calls. Not unusual. A lot of my clients are elderly. The urge to hoard grows with age.

I'd get back to him on the Monday. I try – not always successfully – not to do SpaceWoman work at weekends. I love what I do, but the effort of encouraging people and always sounding positive for them takes a lot out of me. The physical lugging around of boxes and furniture can also be draining. When Friday evening comes round, I'm exhausted, and I need time to recharge my batteries.

I thought that Edward Finch's was just another routine enquiry.

But I didn't know how wrong I could be.

TWO

'There is nothing new under the sun,' he announced. 'Everything comes from somewhere else. Even plastic started off as crude oil or natural gas or coal.'

Dodge is prone to saying things that sound like quotations. Sometimes they are. More often they're his own thoughts. I'd a feeling that, though his last remarks started with a biblical quotation, the rest was pure Dodge. Not too much about plastic in the Bible.

His real name's Gervaise, though I've never heard anyone call him that. In fact, I've rarely heard anyone call him anything. Dodge has a somewhat reclusive personality and I've only seen him with other people in a work context. I think he likes me, though he's never put it into words. Eight years – more than eight years now – we've been working together, and he's never once looked me in the face.

My nickname for him, Dodge, came from Diogenes, the Athenian philosopher whose rejection of consumerism was so strong that it's unfair the way his name has been misapplied in the literature of hoarding. 'Diogenes Syndrome' is used to describe a condition also known as 'senile squalor syndrome', where the elderly surround themselves with rubbish. Most unjust to Diogenes of Sinope, who lived in a large ceramic jar and, very responsibly, kept his possessions to the absolute minimum.

Dodge, though, conforms more accurately to the philosopher's model. Following a private education and a highly lucrative job in the City (from which he retains upper-crust vowels), he suffered some kind of breakdown, the full details of which I have never been told. All I do know is that he emerged from the experience as an enemy of consumerism and a champion of recycling. He has a whole house near the village of Walberton which is full of items he is going to repurpose. And if that sounds like the definition of a hoarder, let me tell you everything there is neatly stacked and catalogued. And, what's more, Dodge does eventually find a way to transform every bit of it into something useful.

He runs a company – of which he is the sole staff member – called 'Treasures Upon Earth'. Its byline is: 'All of your rubbish has a value to someone.'

I was lucky enough to make contact with him, just randomly through an ad in a local free newspaper, soon after I'd started SpaceWoman. It had quickly become clear that I was going to need a reliable 'man with a van' to transport a lot of the clutter I was clearing out of my clients' homes, and Dodge could not have been a more perfect fit for me. Back then, I had assumed most of the household debris would go straight to the dump, but I hadn't reckoned with Dodge's ingenuity and transformational skills.

Which is why I was driving with him that Monday morning in his 1951 Morris Commercial CV9/40 Tipper, a vehicle he maintains with a devotion that almost amounts to worship. And our mission was supplying furniture which Dodge had lovingly constructed from old wooden pallets.

A lot of the work I take on doesn't end with the completion of what was in the job description. Some of my clients, particularly the elderly ones, need a lot of aftercare, and I have to watch it that I don't spend too much unpaid time looking after them.

Mary Griffin was a good example of what I mean. Not elderly in her case, early thirties with a three-year-old daughter called Amy. I'm often employed through social services and charities. I was put on to Mary by a Worthing-based organization that helps in cases of domestic violence.

As a young woman, she had been well placed, owning a two-bedroom house in Ferring, which she had inherited from her parents. She had a job she enjoyed, working as a waitress in Shoreham-on-Sea, and her life appeared to be set fair. Until she met and married the wrong man. Craig Griffin.

The pattern was achingly familiar. Though charming and considerate during the wooing, once married, Craig turned out to be the standard-issue coercive husband, whose manic jealousy had cut Mary off from friends, family, and any form of independent social life. He started to get paranoid about her relationships with the other staff at work and the customers. He took to spending his evenings parked opposite the restaurant where she worked, watching his wife through the glass frontage. If he thought her to have been over-friendly with any of the diners, she would pay for it when she got home. Eventually, Craig's presence became so irksome to her employers that she had to give up the job.

Like many women in such circumstances, sheer terror had prevented Mary from doing anything about his behaviour. She had endured bullying and beatings, even through her pregnancy, and had kept quiet about the situation because she saw no one she dared tell about it. And also, as is so often the case in such situations, she genuinely loved her husband.

Only when he started turning his anger against their daughter did Mary find the courage to speak up and contact the charity. They had acted with commendable speed, informing the police about her husband's violence, and removing Mary and Amy to the safety of a women's refuge. They then embarked on the difficult process of starting legal proceedings against Craig Griffin.

As it turned out, he made things easy for them. In a fury of frustration at his inability to trace his wife, he had refocused his violence on the house. Literally taken a sledgehammer to it. The furniture had been reduced to matchwood and the electrical equipment smashed to pieces. Anything featuring glass – the television, the doors of cupboards, the microwave and the washing machine – had been shattered. When questioned by the police, Craig Griffin did not deny that he was responsible for the destruction. So, he had been arrested for that and was on remand, while the charity's lawyers tried to assemble a case against him for the more serious crime of domestic abuse. As usual, the problem was lack of witnesses. Mary had not been hospitalized after any of her husband's attacks, so there was no paper trail in the medical records. It came down to her word against his. But the lawyers had been in that situation many times before and were hopeful of charging him.

So, Mary had gone from the refuge back to Ferring,

fortunately without Amy the first time, and seen with horror what had happened to their home. That was when I got involved. I'd done other stuff for the charity over the years, but never before had my decluttering skills been required because of criminal damage.

It took a good few trips with Dodge's van to clear it all. And it was a challenge for his considerable powers of recycling. Little had been left in a state where he could repurpose it into something else. Except for some of the large bits of wood. Dodge could always find a use for bits of wood.

Mary was there while I organized the removal of the debris and she did open up to me about her situation. Maybe the time she'd spent in the sympathetic environment of the refuge made her more ready to talk. Maybe it was the knowledge that, at least for a while, Craig couldn't get at her.

The destruction in the house was almost too obvious a symbol for the breakdown of a marriage. Mary felt sufficiently at ease with me to cry as we removed yet another shattered piece of her domestic dreams, though she did try to hold back the tears while Dodge was in the house.

The moment that got to her most was when we started to tidy up Amy's room. The girl's father had shown no mercy with his daughter's possessions. Like most little girls her age, she had been obsessed by the *Frozen* movies, and the floor was littered with the detritus of smashed merchandise – figurines, mugs and hanging ornaments. Craig Griffin had even taken a Stanley knife to Amy's favourite Elsa costume.

But the destruction that hurt Mary most was what had been done to her daughter's bed. The tears poured down unchecked from her brown eyes as she said, 'She was so proud of it. She had just moved into it. No longer a baby's bed. A grown-up little girl's bed. One she could get in and out of at will. She was so proud.'

The tears took over for a moment before she managed to say again, 'So proud. And moving to the grown-up bed coincided with her not needing a nappy at nighttime. She was dry. So proud of being dry. Mind you, that didn't last long, with all the upheaval of going to the refuge. She started bed-wetting there. Back in nappies now.'

Mary sniffed fiercely, hoping to sniff away the tears, as she went on, 'I just hate to think what long-term damage all this has done to Amy. What it's made her think about the things that go on between men and women, whether she'll ever trust a man again. Whether she'll be able to form a decent grown-up relationship herself.'

I didn't give her a reassuring, 'Of course she will.' I knew too much about the effects of childhood trauma to do that. I just said, 'If she needs it later in life, she'll be able to get help.'

'Yes?'

'Yes.'

'I hope so. It took me long enough to ask for help. I just hate the thought of her life being ruined and it being my fault.'

'It won't be your fault. Parents blame themselves too much for what happens to their children. There are lots of other factors in play. Heredity, the education they get, the people they meet, career choices. You haven't any problem loving Amy, have you?'

'No, that's one thing I've never had to worry about.'

'Then she'll come through,' I said.

Dodge, as I said, always finds a use for bits of wood and he's highly creative in what he does with them. When he makes furniture, his basic raw materials are wooden pallets, but other scraps of timber are also pressed into service. He is a wonderfully inventive recycler and, though he sometimes has to buy new screws and nails, he regards paying for anything else as a failure on his part.

Though Dodge didn't look me in the eye when I told him about Mary Griffin's predicament, I could tell he was immediately enthused by the construction project. Everything in the house needed replacing. She hadn't been insured and, though she might eventually get some compensation for the chaos her husband had wreaked, it was going to be a slow process. And she had no income, only a small amount of savings salted away in an account she'd managed to keep secret from Craig. In time, poverty might force her to sell the house and move somewhere smaller, but the charity was determined to prevent that from happening.

So, they helped her replace her shattered possessions, finding a cast-off sofa and some shelves, rugs, mattresses, and bedding. An old electric cooker was sourced, a just-about-working washing machine and a far-from-smart television. For the kitchen, pans, a toaster, and a kettle were unearthed from somewhere.

My first visit after removing the debris, I found that Mary Griffin had hardly started on making the house habitable again. Amy was still being looked after at the refuge, as she had been for some weeks. Mary didn't want the little girl to see the destruction her father had wrought. But she herself didn't seem to be capable of making the effort required to recreate her home. All the stuff delivered by the charity still lay where they had put it down. For Mary, the effort of moving it seemed too great.

I recognized how traumatized she was. And knew that I would have to hold her hand through every step of the reorganization process. That morning I arranged for a plumber and electrician to do the necessary work on the kitchen appliances and guided Mary in moving the piled-up furniture into the relevant rooms.

On top of the charity's donations of furniture, Dodge had contributed stuff he'd already made, tables and chairs, whose finely sanded and oiled finish would never have betrayed their humble origin as pallets.

But his new project, on which he spent God knows how many hours, was a bed for Amy. Not quite full-size but big enough for her to think of it as grown-up.

That was what we were driving to deliver at Mary Griffin's house the Monday morning he quoted Ecclesiastes at me. The bed lay in flat-pack form, covered with a blanket in the back of his van, ready to be assembled when we got there.

He took the makings of the bed upstairs while Mary and I lingered over coffee in the kitchen. With my help and encouragement, she had managed to get all the furniture into the right rooms. The plumber and electrician I'd organized had fixed her a working kitchen. There was still plenty left to do

– pegged-up sheets substituted for curtains and so on – but the place was beginning to look like a home again.

So much so that Mary had taken the decision to bring Amy back that afternoon and was clearly worried about the likely response. The little girl had witnessed many traumatic scenes in the house and its new improvised furnishings would be unfamiliar to her.

I was about to reassure Mary when we heard a cough and turned to see the tall figure of Dodge in the doorway. Needless to say, he didn't look at either of us as he mumbled that, if we wanted to come upstairs, the bed was ready for inspection.

It was his masterwork. Solid, very definitely grown-up, and painted pink. A little girl's dream – and with a refinement to warm Amy's heart.

I must have mentioned the movie *Frozen* to Dodge because I'm sure he'd never heard of it before. His spartan living quarters did not contain a television and he never mentioned going out to the cinema. Nor do I think he ever bought newspapers or magazines.

But somehow, he'd known what was needed. On the bed's headboard was a row of *Frozen* stickers.

'Oh!' exclaimed Mary, tears glinting in her tired eyes. 'That is so fabulous! Oh, I must give you a hug!'

But, intuitively recognizing Dodge's uneasiness about human contact, she didn't carry out her intention.

'No worries,' he mumbled in his awkward, privately schooled accent. 'I'll make some more stuff for her, dressing table and what-have-you.'

Turning to me, Mary said, 'Amy will be over the moon about the bed. I can't thank you – I can't thank both of you enough!'

A shadow of doubt crossed her face. 'I hope it'll be all right,' she said. 'I just hope to God it'll be all right.'

I saw the fear in her eye. Sentences for the kind of crimes her husband committed can sometimes be excessively lenient. Whether she and Amy would be allowed to continue to live peacefully in their house once Craig had been released . . . well, no one could predict that.

I had a feeling Mary Griffin might be on my unpaid books for quite a time to come.

I'd left the Yeti at Dodge's. He was silent as we drove back. 'Everything all right?' I asked.

'Yes, yes,' he replied vaguely. And I realized the limitations of my knowledge of him. There were substantial areas of his past and his current life which he never talked about. I respected that and never probed. If he wanted to share something with me, that was his decision.

But I got the feeling that something was upsetting him.

I was on my way back to Chichester when I remembered a call I hadn't made. I stopped in a layby and keyed in the number.

'Hello?'

The word had a questioning tone. I immediately recognized the voice from the message left over the weekend.

'Mr Finch, it's Ellen Curtis of SpaceWoman. Returning your call.'

'Oh, thank you very much for getting back to me.' He somehow sounded surprised that I had.

There was a silence. 'So, how can I help you?' I prompted.

'Ah. Well. Yes. The fact is . . . I gather you help people who've sort of . . . let things get on top of them. That is . . . I meant literal things, objects, stuff. I didn't mean letting "things get on top of them" in the emotional sense.'

I could have told him that very often the two came together, but it wasn't the moment. 'You're right. That's what I do. "Decluttering and Interior Restyling" it says on my card.'

'Yes, yes, I saw that.'

'Sorry, do you mind if I ask where you saw it?' It's important that I know where I'm getting enquiries from. 'Online?'

'Oh, no, no,' he said in a tone confirming my earlier impression that he wasn't at the sharp end of modern technology. 'No, a friend looked up the listings or whatever you call them. In a newspaper, I assume. And she recommended you because you were local.'

'Right. So, do you mind if I ask where you are based?'

'I'm in Lancing. I have a bungalow in Lancing.' No surprise. Bungalows are spread like a rash along the South Coast.

'Not too far away,' I said. 'That's fine.'

Another silence required a further prompt from me. 'And you're finding you're rather drowning in stuff . . . is that the problem?'

'Exactly that. "Drowning in stuff" – very apposite, a very good way of putting it.'

'Well, maybe I should come and have a look at your place, see what I can do to help you?'

'Oh, would you be prepared to do that?' He sounded surprised.

'That's what my job is,' I said. 'And, incidentally, you won't be charged anything for the first visit.'

'That's very kind,' he said, again surprised.

'Well, let's get the details, where you are and when it would be convenient to come and visit you.'

I had been promising myself that I would catch up with sending out some invoices that afternoon, just ahead of my accountant badgering me about it. But I'd always rather be out doing the practical part of the job than the paperwork, so we fixed that I'd go to Edward Finch's place at two.

As we were nearing the end of the call, I asked, 'Is this problem of clutter something you've been dealing with for a long time?'

'Well,' he replied, 'I've never been the tidiest of people, but . . . I think things have got a lot worse since my wife died.'

It's so often the case that hoarding behaviour is triggered by bereavement. I identified Edward Finch's type; a widower whose grief paralysed any tidying-up instinct he might have possessed. A straightforward, standard-issue case.

How wrong could I be?

THREE

E dward Finch was not one of those hoarders whose problem you would recognize from outside their homes. The front garden of his Lancing bungalow was well maintained, the gate neatly painted black, and no weeds allowed to assert themselves between the red bricks of the front path. The exterior was only distinguishable from all of the others in the road by choice of paintwork and curtains.

The interior, though, was another matter. As I could see as soon as he opened the front door.

He opened it wide, which was unusual. Many hoarders are resistant to letting anyone into their space. Even people they're expecting. Many's the appointment I've made which didn't happen because the client wouldn't allow me in. In some cases, I've had to go through a kind of wooing process, turning up every day for a week until I was finally granted admission. Occasionally, that moment never arrived and, if there was a Health and Safety issue, the police would have to take a battering ram to the front door.

Those who do let me in often take a long time to come to the door and then peer through a crack with the chain still in place. Edward Finch had no such inhibitions.

What the opened door revealed in the hall was untidiness but not squalor. Nor did I get the blast of smell for which I always prepare myself at a new property. I immediately removed the sharp-proof gloves which I wear as a precautionary measure on a first visit.

The walls of the hall were piled high with sagging cardboard boxes whose contents I could only guess at. They were teetering towards the ceiling and probably a bit wobbly but not an immediate danger (depending of course on how heavy their contents were). I've seen much worse. There was a clear path between them and the exposed carpet had been recently vacuumed.

Edward Finch did not look too far gone either. When I meet a new client, I have to be prepared for anything. Some hoarders are literally unaware of their appearance and, never seeing anyone, don't make any concessions to personal hygiene. But he wasn't like that.

A small, neat man with a good head of well-cut grey hair, he had shaved that morning. His brown eyes looked innocent, exposed almost, ready to flinch at any adversity. He wore a khaki quilted gilet over an open-necked tattersall shirt and light brown needlecord trousers.

'Mrs Curtis, so good of you to come.' As he had on the phone, he sounded almost surprised that I was fulfilling the agreement to visit him. I was only doing my job, after all.

'My pleasure,' I said. There was not exactly an awkward silence, but a vague one. He looked at me as if he had been expecting someone quite different. 'May I come in?' I asked.

'Yes, yes, of course. Sorry, forgetting my manners.' He ushered me in and closed the front door behind me.

Again, a moment of indecision. Then, 'Can I offer you a tea or coffee?'

'Oh, thank you. A coffee'd be lovely.'

'Would you mind coming through to the kitchen while I make it? I'd show you into the sitting room but it's a bit of a glory hole.'

From what I could gather of the bungalow's layout, the living room and kitchen were to the right of the hall. To the left presumably there were two bedrooms and a bathroom.

The kitchen was chaotic too, but again it was organized chaos. No smell here either, no rotting food. Yes, a lot of instant meal cartons, but all stacked up in an orderly fashion. And no unwashed crockery in the sink. Either Edward had an intrinsic sense of tidiness or he had someone who came in to help him keep the right side of total dysfunction.

The kettle he filled and the mugs he brought down from a cupboard were clean. 'Sorry, it's instant. Is that OK?'

'Fine.'

'Milk or sugar?'

'Dash of milk, please.'

He made the drinks, putting two heaped teaspoons of sugar

into his own. As he passed my mug across, he said, 'Right, brace yourself for the worst.' And he led the way back into the hall and opened the door of the sitting room.

Yes, again it was a mess, but nothing that I couldn't have sorted out in a couple of hours with some cardboard boxes and binbags. Not a hoarder's accumulation of stuff, more just evidence of laziness, and of the fact that this was the home of a book-lover. They were scattered all over the place. Also, magazines and newspapers left open, a few discarded garments, shoes shuffled off on to the floor while watching television. Nothing that would decompose. Not even any encrusted coffee cups on the mantelpiece.

I looked around the room and shrugged. 'This isn't bad,' I said. 'I don't think you have a big problem, Mr Finch.'

'Oh, please call me Edward.'

'Very well, Edward,'

'My friends call me Eddie.'

'Well, let's stick with Edward, for the time being, shall we?' I wasn't being standoffish; I just like keeping things professional.

'Very well.'

He looked slightly hurt, so I said, 'And you call me Ellen.'

'Right.' That seemed to cheer him.

'As I say, I don't really see a major hoarding problem here. Just think you need to get into the habit of putting things away when you've finished with them.'

'Hm.' He nodded thoughtfully and took a sip from his coffee. 'Of course,' he said, 'you haven't seen the bedrooms yet.'

'No, that's true. I haven't.'

He led me across the hall to where I'd assumed the sleeping quarters would be. Spare bedroom facing the front with a door through to the bathroom, from which another door led back to the master bedroom (if you can actually have a 'master bedroom' in a bungalow). That had a second door opening on to the hall.

The spare room was untidy in the way that a student's room might be. Books, papers scattered on every surface, clothes twisted into humanoid shapes as they'd been discarded on to the floor. Laptop and television perched on top of stuff on the dressing table. The bed was unmade.

'This is where I'm currently sleeping,' said Edward Finch. 'Come through.'

There were towels on the bathroom floor, but the ceramic surfaces had all recently been wiped clean.

'This is where the problem really is,' he said as he opened the door to the back bedroom.

I saw what he meant. The wardrobe doors were open, and their contents spread literally over everything. Dresses, trouser suits, underwear, make-up, scattered on the double bed, bedside tables, dressing table, chairs. Here there was a smell, not a revolting one, just the clinging odour of stale perfume.

Everything that belonged to Edward Finch's wife was there. Everything except for the woman herself.

He turned to face me. Tears glinted in the innocent brown eyes. 'I can't move it,' he said. 'I keep trying and I . . . just can't move it.'

This was a problem I'd encountered many times before. Bereavement affects people in different ways. Some immediately remove every trace of the deceased, hoping that will kill the memories. Some physically distance themselves, moving house as quickly as possible. Others, like Edward Finch, find removing the belongings of the departed more than they can cope with. I've known cases where the bereaved haven't moved a single item for ten years or longer.

'I understand, Edward,' I said. 'The way you're reacting is quite common, after the loss of a loved one. And I know that at the moment the task seems insurmountable, but I promise you I can help you achieve it.'

'As you have helped other people?' There was a new edge of cynicism in his voice.

'Exactly. As I have helped other people.'

'Yes, but I'm not like other people.'

'No, everyone is different. I'm sure we can find a way to—'

'Other people didn't kill their wives, did they?' said Edward Finch.

FOUR

I didn't think he was telling the truth. I don't mean that he was deliberately lying, just that he was confused, that bereavement wasn't allowing him to think straight. He may have felt guilty about his wife's death – that's a very common reaction – but I didn't think he'd caused it. Anyway, I certainly wasn't about to pass on what Edward Finch had told me to the police.

So, I ignored his pronouncement, which seemed rather to annoy him, as if he felt cheated of further interrogation. I suggested we should make an appointment for me to come and start the clearance required. That seemed to cheer him up and I went through the ritual of telling him my charges and terms of business. My view was that spending more time with Edward Finch might help me understand why he'd come up with a confession of murder. And help me to judge whether there was any element of truth in the claim.

Anyway, we fixed that I would do a working visit to him the day after next, the Wednesday.

I'd been in the bungalow for less than half an hour, so there was nothing to stop me from returning to face the reproachful invoices in Chichester. I had only just got in the Yeti and turned on the ignition when my mobile rang.

'Hello?'

'Is that SpaceWoman?'

'Yes. You're talking to Ellen Curtis.' I always answered like that. Not to give the impression that I managed a huge staff, just to open up the possibility of a first-name conversation.

'You don't know me. My name's Cara Reece. And I believe you've just been visiting Edward Finch.'

I looked along the row of near-identical bungalows. Behind which untwitching curtains did the spy lurk?

'Yes. Yes, I have,' I confirmed.

'He told me you were coming. I was so glad.'

'Sorry, I'm not quite sure who you are.'

'I'm a friend of Eddie's. We used to teach at the same school.'

'Ah. Thank you.'

'And I was the one who persuaded him to contact you. You know, I looked online for a suitable person to help him and you seemed to fit the bill . . . sorry, is it Mrs Curtis or Miss Curtis?'

'Mrs.'

'So, you're married?'

This was an odd thing to say and the way she said it was odd too. Almost with relief. I found myself saying, 'I'm a widow.' Which is unlike me. Normally, I keep my personal information to a minimum at work. I moved on quickly. 'Anyway, call me Ellen.'

'Oh. Thank you. Then please call me Cara.'

'Fine. Cara it is.'

'What I really wanted to ask, Ellen, is: Do you think you can help him?'

'Yes, I think I can.'

'I'm so pleased. He was so totally devastated when Pauline died.'

Good to have a name. It struck me that Edward hadn't mentioned that detail.

'I mean,' Cara went on, 'I've done what I could to help . . . you know, run a Hoover over things, cooked him the odd meal . . .' That explained the relative tidiness of the bungalow. 'But increasingly I've been coming round to the idea that Eddie needs professional help . . . which is why I got him to contact you.'

'I'm glad you did, Cara.'

'I wasn't sure whether it was practical help he needed or, you know, psychological . . .?'

I didn't tell her how close the two were. I just said, 'I'll start with getting the practical stuff sorted. Then we'll see what kind of a state he's in, whether he needs more specialized help.'

'Thank you. I'm so relieved that he let you in.'

'Sorry?'

'Eddie's very volatile. Sometimes he won't let me in the

house, even if I've made an arrangement to see him. Sometimes he doesn't even answer his phone. He knows how worried I get about that.'

What she said made me wonder if there was another side to Edward Finch, capable of using his mental state to exercise power over Cara. Her tone of voice suggested she was almost frightened of him. Subservient, certainly. He wouldn't be the first time I'd encountered the phenomenon of an ineffectual control freak.

There were interesting depths to the relationship between Edward Finch and Cara Reece. Interesting for a psychologist, that is, not depths I needed to investigate. Not at that point, anyway.

'As I said,' Cara went on – I got the feeling she was a bit of a talker, 'I'm so pleased that you're going to be helping Eddie. If I give you my number, will you keep me up to date with how things go?'

'Assume they're fine unless you hear from me.' I said this for reasons of client confidentiality. My work often leads to the uncovering of personal secrets which should not be spread around. Like, say, someone confessing to having murdered his wife.

Maybe Cara's thoughts were moving in the same direction, because she asked, rather anxiously, 'Eddie didn't say anything to you, did he . . . about the circumstances of Pauline's death . . .?'

'No,' I lied cheerfully.

I ended the conversation with Cara but was frustrated from driving off by another phone call.

'Hi, it's Alexandra Richards.' She sounded so much more animated than she had on our previous encounter that I hardly recognized her voice. Before I could say anything, she went on, 'I've talked to Ingrid and she's happy to see you.'

'Oh, well done. Will you be there?'

'No. She says she wants it to be just the two of you when she interviews you.'

'Oh, I see.' I was amused. 'She's going to interview me, is she?'

Alexandra didn't answer that. She said, 'Could you make it this evening?'

I had no plans beyond cooking myself something and a bit of random television, so I agreed. 'You said she lives in Brighton . . .?'

She gave me the address in Brunswick Square. Hove technically, of course, rather than Brighton. Not cheap, though. Top-floor apartment in one of those lovely old Grade I Regency houses built round the central garden on three sides and facing the sea.

'Would six o'clock be all right for you, Ellen?'

'I could do that, yes.'

'One thing . . .' Alexandra added.

'Yes?'

'Do you drink?'

'Why do you ask?'

'Because she does.'

I hadn't got anything else booked until my meeting – or should I say 'interview' – with Ingrid Richards. I reminded myself to check her out on Wikipedia when I got back. Alexandra had said her mother was famous, and the name did ring a distant bell, so I should at least do some basic research.

But when I reached home, I got diverted by the bloody invoices – not too many overdue, but they still needed doing. I am actually quite organized, and the accountant rarely has to bully me about paperwork. I'm good with money and got better with it when I was looking after the business side of Oliver's work. But I cannot claim that I find it the most interesting part of the job. I dream of a time when SpaceWoman might have a finance director, but I know it's never going to happen. I'm a one-woman band and, actually, I'm not sure that I'd like being joined by other musicians.

Being at home somehow made me think about ringing Ben, and round four thirty I gave in to the temptation.

I got his voicemail. As I had done the last few times I'd tried. I left a message, 'Wondering what planet you're on. Contact mother ship. Lots of love.'

I didn't ask what I wanted to ask. 'Are you all right? Or are you depressed?'

I don't enjoy worrying about Ben as much as I do. He's a grown man, for God's sake. And he seemed currently to have an ongoing girlfriend. Tracey. I know how some mothers react to their precious sons developing girlfriends, but I can honestly say I wasn't at all jealous. I was just glad he'd got someone.

And I didn't mind him not ringing me if he was spending all his time with her. If he was happy.

If he *was* happy . . .?

Fleur had been right . . . as she had an annoying habit of sometimes being right, just when I was getting most exasperated with her. It did worry me that Ben hadn't introduced Tracey.

Such thoughts – and the invoices – preoccupied me. When I next checked the time, I realized I was in danger of being late for my rendezvous – interview? – in Brighton. I rushed out of the house.

FIVE

'Do you drink whiskey?' Ingrid Richards demanded as soon as I got through the door. 'I start drinking whiskey at six p.m. It is my aim not to drink any earlier in the day. That's an ambition in which I frequently fail.'

'I'll have a glass with you. Thank you,' I said.

Normally, as I say, on my first visit to a client's home, I would wear sharp-proof gloves, never knowing what level of squalor or safety I would be faced with. But I was glad I hadn't put them on for Ingrid. It was clear that, at this stage at least, she wanted our meeting to have the appearance of a purely social encounter.

The first thing that struck me about Ingrid Richards was her face. Though fine-boned, rather beautiful in shape, under a layer of freckles its skin was criss-crossed by a thousand tiny lines. It looked like old leather. It was the face of someone who had spent a lot of time exposed to the sun in hot countries and whose constant smoking had contributed to the tanning process.

On her forehead there was a scar. At least two inches long, the wound that had left it must have been deep. Maybe the kind of gash you get from hitting the windscreen in a car crash?

There was a Gauloise hanging from her lips when she opened the door. It stayed there as she gestured me to an armchair and went across to the open kitchen area to organize the drinks. The flat was on the eastern side of the square. The tall windows offered a good view of the sea. A May evening, sun sparkling on the water with a promise of summer.

Around the room I saw a collage of exotic items. On the walls hung Russian icons, Islamic ceramic tiles, silk pictures and tapestries. On shelves and other surfaces stood a samovar, a folding Koran stand, brass bowls, trays and candlesticks, chased silver boxes and Ottoman vases. I remembered

Alexandra telling me that her mother had lived 'all over the bloody world'.

'I drink my whiskey neat,' Ingrid called across to me. 'Do you want ice or water or anything else with it?'

'Happy with it neat,' I replied.

I don't dislike spirits, just very rarely drink them. In fact, I like most alcohol and there have been times in my life – certainly my 'ladette' late twenties – when I drank far too much of the stuff. A lot of drinking was involved when I first got together with Oliver too, mostly red wine back then. The genuine reason for my current moderation – as I keep telling my mother, though she never believes me – is that losing my licence would kill the SpaceWoman business stone dead.

I'm also glad that the same fear stops me from drinking too much on my own at home. The occasional large Merlot and that's it. I've seen from my work how easily the drinking can build up along with the hoarding. With sufficient alcohol in your system, you cease to notice the chaos of your surroundings. And, for a while, cease to feel the pain of whatever started you hoarding in the first place.

Reading between the lines of what Alexandra told me, I'd deduced that her mother would chat more freely to someone she was having a drink with, and had planned the evening accordingly. I left the Yeti at home and came by train. There's a rackety service that runs along the coast from Portsmouth Harbour to Brighton, stopping conveniently at Chichester – and at more South Coast villages than you would imagine a cartographer could invent. Most of them end with 'ing' – Angmering, Goring, Worthing, Lancing, et cetera. And, more importantly, there's a station at Hove.

Ingrid handed me whiskey in a squat, thick-bottomed glass. '*Slánte!*' she said, clicking hers against mine before taking a grateful slurp.

'*Slánte!*' I echoed, following suit, mildly intrigued as to why she used the Irish toast. Though it was a while since I'd drunk the stuff, I was surprised by the taste. Sweeter than I was expecting.

Ingrid read my reaction. 'We're drinking "whiskey" with an "e",' she explained. 'Irish. Jameson's.'

'Fine by me,' I said.

She arranged her long limbs on a hard wooden chair, which she'd turned around to face away from her desk, on which an open laptop and an overspilling ashtray perched on layers of paper. A mixture of books, diaries, and browning newspaper clippings. These spread from the desktop over the floor, then into separate piles on other surfaces, in what a casual observer might have seen as chaos. Experience had told me, though, that it could well be an efficient personal filing system, whose originator could instantly find any relevant document. Untidiness does not always indicate lack of control.

If that was how Ingrid Richards wanted to organize her work, fine. From the Health and Safety point of view, though, perhaps not so good.

In spite of her weather-beaten skin and the scar, Ingrid remained a fine-looking woman. Casually dressed in a floppy white linen shirt and well-cut jeans, she certainly had style. And, though in her seventies, her long slender figure was almost girlish.

Then there was the hair. Red. And the residual freckles suggested it had always been red. Surely no longer unaided, but she'd employed a highly skilled colourist.

The more I saw of Ingrid Richards, the more familiar she looked. Alexandra had told me her mother was famous and I was kicking myself for not Wikipediaing her before I left home.

Ingrid looked me directly in the eyes. I got the feeling she hadn't got another way of looking at people. 'Obviously, I know why you're here,' she said. Her voice was firm and confident, occasionally slackening to something approaching American. She went on, 'At the behest of my censorious daughter.'

'Is she censorious?'

'Oh, I think so. Most of that generation are. Do you have children?'

'Two. Girl and boy, in that order.'

'And is your daughter censorious?'

'No, I don't think I'd call her that.'

'Then what would you call her?'

'Self-sufficient, maybe . . .? Uncommunicative, certainly.'

'Hm.' She screwed up her eyes. They were, I'd noticed, amber-coloured, flecked with something darker. Lion's eyes. 'I sometimes wish Alexandra would show a bit more self-sufficiency.'

I was about to respond but Ingrid got in her question first. I saw why I had been told that the encounter would be an interview. 'Are you married to the father of your children?'

'I was,' I replied.

'"Was"? Divorced?'

'He died.'

'Ah. And what did he do before he died?'

'He was a cartoonist.'

'Would I have heard of him?'

'His name's Oliver Curtis.' I still had a problem putting his life into the past tense.

She shook her head. The name meant nothing to her.

Instinctively, I went to Oliver's defence. 'He did the "Major Cock-Ups" strip. And "Teddy Blair". "Riq and Raq" . . .?'

'God, yes. I remember those. Very sharp. He understood politics. Really got under the skin of those losers Major and Blair.' She looked at me with new respect for a moment, then quickly moved on. 'I married twice. It didn't take. Either time.'

'Ah.'

'You show remarkable restraint,' Ingrid observed perceptively, 'in not asking which of my husbands contributed to Alexandra's appearance.'

I didn't deny that that was what I had been wondering.

'Well, it was neither of the *husbands*,' she said, larding the word with contempt, 'but there's no secret about it. Are there any secrets at all in these days of Wikipedia?'

I felt even more guilty for not having looked her up.

'Alexandra,' she went on, 'was the result of a brief and ill-advised skirmish with Niall Connor.'

She said the name as if I ought to know it. And it did sound familiar, though I couldn't be sure of the context. To do with newspapers perhaps . . .?

I was reminded of something Oliver was always saying. Having for some years contributed cartoon strips to the national dailies, he knew a lot about the Press. He liked the buzz of that world, frequently got into long drinking sessions with journalists. But he often told me that, as a profession, they overrated themselves. 'Think they're much more important than they are. All tin-pot junior reporters see themselves as Carl Bernstein and Bob Woodward in *All the President's Men*, bringing down governments by their fearless investigations. Changing history – huh. Whereas the average journalist is just an unoriginal hack with a drinking problem.

'And the fuss they make when one of their number dies. Journalists always get a disproportionate amount of obituary space. As if they're really important. And very few of them are even mildly important. Except to each other.'

I felt the unblinking focus of Ingrid Richards' lion eyes on me. 'Niall Connor the journalist?' I hazarded, hopefully not about to sound stupid if it turned out to be another Niall Connor.

'Yes. Niall Connor the *journalist*.' It was a different kind of contempt she put into that word. Somehow more personal than the way she had disparaged her husbands.

'Niall didn't believe in marriage,' she went on. 'Or perhaps I should say that he didn't believe in marriage until he got married. To Grace Bellamy, of all people.'

That was a name I did recognize. She was one of those women who had views on everything and shared them with the public through a regular column in the *Daily Mail*, along with frequent radio and television appearances. She had also been a regular presence in lifestyle magazines for decades.

'I know who you mean,' I said. 'Another journalist.'

'Hardly a journalist,' Ingrid sneered. 'A Dial-An-Opinion slot machine, maybe? One of those sickening women who is professionally positive. All the bloody time. Something to say on every subject, gets a column out of everything that comes into her life. Do you know, she actually wrote a book about her own menopause? For God's sake! As if it'd never happened to anyone else. That's not journalism, not real journalism. In fact, it's hard to think of a lower form of literary endeavour.

'Do you know, Grace Bellamy once tried to set up an interview with me? Don't know how she'd got my contacts, but I suppose you can get anything online these days. She'd done her research – or got someone to do the research for her. She knew where I lived, she knew something of my habits – the Gauloises, the Jameson's – don't know how she found all that out, but I suppose plenty's been written about me in the past, easy enough for a researcher to access.

'Anyway, she rang me, asked if she could write a feature on me for one of the Sunday supplements – can't remember which one it was. Right wing, anyway, that's her kind of demographic. I politely thanked her very much but said I didn't like having my name associated with *lightweight tabloid journalism!*' She chuckled with relish at the remembered put-down.

'So,' she went on, 'I find it rather sad that Niall ended up married to a woman like that. He was always a bastard, but he used to have some integrity. About his work, anyway. Not about much else. He may not have believed in marriage till he reached middle age, but he certainly believed in infidelity. Which, strangely, is the one subject Grace Bellamy hasn't written a column about. Yet. Maintaining the front of the everything-in-the-garden's-lovely marriage, I dare say. Doesn't want to threaten their *domestic bliss.*' More pure venom.

'Some wives, I'm told, can close their minds to their husbands' infidelities. Which must be a very necessary ability for anyone married to a predatory pouncer like Niall. He was always the same. God, I've spent enough times in war zones with him to witness him in action. He'd make a grab at anything with breasts and a pulse.

'Which, all right, may not say much for my taste that I went to bed with him. But he did have an undeniable something, particularly back then. And when you're stuck out somewhere like Beirut in the 1980s, never knowing whether you'd see the end of the next day . . . well, a sort of blitz mentality develops. The Commodore Hotel witnessed many unlikelier couplings than me and Niall.

'Still, I dare say age has slowed him down a bit by now. Difficult to recapture the spontaneity of a predatory pouncer when you have to wait an hour for the Viagra to kick in.'

I was quite surprised by the vitriol Ingrid Richards directed towards her former lover and his wife. From her detached, even sceptical manner, I'd expected her to present a more woman-of-the-world response to romantic disappointments. But Niall Connor had clearly got under skin, as well as under her duvet, and had hurt her deeply.

I felt the time had arrived when I could say something. 'When Alexandra talked to me, she gave the impression that her father hadn't played much of a part in her life.'

'No. The only part he played was impregnating me. And he didn't know he'd achieved that until a long time after the event. He'd lost interest in me long before he knew Alexandra existed. I don't think he ever had much interest in her.'

'And was she resentful of that?'

Ingrid shrugged. 'I would assume so, but I don't really know. I never found it easy to find out what Alexandra was thinking.'

'What about now?'

'How do you mean?'

'Do you find it any easier to know what she's thinking now she's an adult?'

'God, no. Harder than ever.' She turned the lion's eyes on me with disarming frankness. 'Look, I really don't know much about Alexandra. I've never spent any length of time with her. It's only recently that she's insisted on being in touch on a regular basis. Looking after me – that's probably the way she sees it. God save me from that! And I suppose her bringing you in to check me out is part of her mistaken mission of mercy.

'Listen, I've been a crap mother, no two ways about it. I'm not claiming any brownie points on that score. I never wanted to have a child and, as a result, I've probably messed up Alexandra's life completely.'

I tried to imagine Fleur ever saying the same about me but couldn't see it. She was far too well armoured in self-esteem to entertain such thoughts. I don't think it ever occurred to Fleur Bonnier that she'd ever done anything wrong, certainly not in her upbringing of me. To her mind, the only blemish in our relationship is that I'm not sufficiently appreciative of my good fortune in having Fleur Bonnier as a mother.

Ingrid went on, 'I was stupid. I'd fallen pregnant a couple of times before in my life and had abortions – no problem. With her . . . well, circumstances meant that that was not an option. And, once I'd taken the pregnancy on board, I started to think . . . I was in my early forties, last-chance saloon possibly, and the work wasn't going that well. I had been injured and out of it for a while. So, I wondered whether maybe I should be looking for something else in my life . . . though God knows why I thought a baby would be the answer. The chances of my having a total personality transplant at that age . . . well, there's an old proverb about leopards and spots, isn't there?

'So, I'm afraid I brought into the world – and shamefully neglected – this poor lump of a girl who has no desire to be distinguished in any way. No ambition. I just can't get my head around that. She wants the world to be totally unaware she's even in it. I tell you there's no parapet so low that Alexandra wouldn't hide her head behind it.'

'Do you think it's possible,' I suggested, 'that she's turned out so self-effacing because you have such a high profile?'

'Oh, well done.' She fixed the eyes on me again. 'What are you, Ellen – a declutterer or a psychologist?'

'Sometimes have to be a bit of both.'

She nodded, assessing what I'd said and deciding she approved. Then she sighed. 'I feel sorry for Alexandra. Sorry that the poor kid ended up with me as a mother. Almost anyone else would have done the job better.'

This wasn't said with self-pity. Or self-condemnation. Just acceptance of one of life's inevitabilities.

SIX

'**A**nd the neglected child,' Ingrid Richards went on, 'about whose welfare I never worried nearly enough, is now worried about me.'

'Yes.'

'I hope she didn't suggest to you that I might be demented?'

'She didn't, no. She was very clear on that point.'

'Good. I can assure you that all of my marbles are firmly in place. And will be so long as I keep working. But, so long as I have my work and my health . . .'

'How is your health?'

'Much better than it has any right to be.' To emphasize the point, she took a long swallow of whiskey, nearly draining the glass, stubbed out the remains of her Gauloise and lit another one. 'I've been kippering myself with the fags and the Jameson's for a long time now. One day I'll get cancer or have a stroke. Then, if I have the misfortune to survive, I'll probably have to make adjustments to my lifestyle. Till then, I will continue to live tamely in Brighton . . . or Hove, to be strictly accurate. "Hove, actually", as everyone round here rather waggishly puts it. Not quite the heady days of the eighties and the Groucho Club. But on the plus side – or is it a minus – no bombs in Brighton since the biggie that nearly put paid to Thatcher in 1984, no shellfire, and the only invasions are by day-trippers.'

Of course! How stupid I'd been not to recognize the name. Now I knew exactly who Ingrid Richards was. I should have recognized her from the distinctive scar. She had been a fixture on our television screens for decades. Not so much in the last ten years, but up until then, wherever the wars were fiercest, that's where Ingrid Richards was to be found. Jokes used to float around, as some new international crisis emerged. 'Oh, it must be serious. They've sent Ingrid Richards out there.'

And I remembered the outline details of how she got the

scar. It was a war wound, a badge of honour, sustained in some hellhole. Beirut, I think it was. Ingrid Richards had been out there sometime in the 1980s, which of course would have been when she got together with Niall Connor. They were both in Lebanon covering a civil war, was it . . .? I'm sorry, I'm not very good on the history of the Middle East. But I seem to recall that Ingrid was with a cameraman, covering the conflict for the BBC, and they were too near to a car bomb which was detonated . . .? Something like that. Both of them were hit by shrapnel – that's when she got the head injury. Then I think Ingrid Richards was brought back to the UK and hospitalized for quite a while . . .

What I do know for certain is that the dent in her forehead became part of her image, a constant reminder to the nation's viewers of the dangers she had survived.

I couldn't remember details of her private life, but I seemed to remember it was fairly rackety. A couple of marriages, as she'd just confirmed. Certainly, a few high-profile lovers. Amongst them, I now knew, Niall Connor, to whom she owed the dubious gift of Alexandra. What else? Even more, I wished I'd at least read the Wikipedia entry.

'We need more whiskey,' Ingrid announced, reaching out for my glass. Her own was empty.

I downed the remaining contents and handed mine across. I'm not the sort to get into competitive drinking but I knew refusal might threaten the atmosphere of intimate chat that was building up between us.

'You've never smoked?' she called across from where she was pouring the drinks.

'No. Didn't like the taste, while all my contemporaries were looking dead sophisticated with fags drooping out of their mouths. I looked even less confident with a cigarette than I did without one.' I didn't add that I was grateful that I'd never started. Didn't want to sound pious.

'You don't know what you're missing,' said Ingrid, handing me a nearly full tumbler of Jameson's. 'People often ask me what it feels like waking up in a war zone, not knowing if I'll still be alive at the end of the day. And I tell them, "It's all right, so long as I can get a cigarette first thing."'

The words would have sounded boastful from most people but, coming from her, they didn't. She had lived that life and was justified in talking about it.

'Anyway,' she moved on, 'I agreed to see you because Alexandra wanted me to. Now we've met – what?' She answered her own question before I had the chance. 'You're going to tell me that this place is a fire hazard – right?'

'Probably.'

'And I'm going to say, "Thank you very much for your opinion, Ellen Curtis, but I have no intention of making any changes." The fact is that, in spite of my daughter's solicitude and conviction that I'm losing my marbles, I'm extremely careful about my personal safety. My experience of war zones has taught me how to avoid avoidable risks. There are no doubt people out there who'd like to kill me – I've rubbed a lot of people up the wrong way in the course of my career – but there's no way I'll die by accident.

'And if Alexandra has told you that I fall into bed every night, smashed out of my skull, she is wrong. I remain in control and sleep well. One thing my life has trained me for is the ability to sleep anywhere and to sleep instantly. I've never had any need of sleeping pills.

'The trouble is that Alexandra doesn't realize how inured I have become to the effects of alcohol. It doesn't affect my faculties and I don't get hangovers. Drinking late into the night – vodka in Chechnya, arak in Syria, whiskey more or less anywhere – has been part of my professional way of life. I've elicited more useful information over booze than I ever would have done over cups of tea – and still been able to file perfect copy in the morning. So, Alexandra doesn't need to worry on that score.'

She gestured around the paper-filled room. 'This is how I live. This is how I want to live. And it suits me.'

She looked at me defiantly, expecting counter-arguments, but I produced none. She grinned.

'Right, Ellen. So, our business is concluded. Were you the kind of person I thought you'd be when Alexandra said she'd arranged for you to visit, I would now be saying, "Piss off out of here!"'

'Right,' I said, reaching for my handbag.

She raised her hand to stop me. 'Since, however, you turn out to be intelligent and congenial, I'm very happy to continue sitting here drinking with you until you need to get back home . . . wherever your home may be.'

'Chichester.'

'Right.' She looked at me, almost appealing, vulnerable for the first time in our encounter. 'So . . .?'

'Well,' I said, 'since you have just filled my glass to the brim with Jameson's, I think it would be a waste for me to leave the rest of it and go straight away.'

'Don't worry about that,' said Ingrid with a crooked smile. 'I will happily finish up your leftovers.'

'Very generous of you, but I think I'd rather finish them up myself.'

'Excellent.' The crooked grin turned into a broad smile. 'So, tell me how you got into the decluttering? Bit of a niche business, isn't it?'

It struck me, as I described the genesis of SpaceWoman, what a good interviewer Ingrid Richards was. Of course, that had been part of her job, one of the most important parts of her job, right through her career. It was her business to get people to reveal the truth. Under her gentle prompting, I found I was giving out much more detail – much more personal detail – than I would when normally asked about my work.

Also, she sounded genuinely interested. I remember somebody famous – I can't remember who it was – saying that the first essential for a journalist is curiosity. And Ingrid Richards was profoundly curious. She wanted to know about everything she didn't already know about. Unlike most people, who only ask me about my work as a bridge to the next thing they want to talk about.

I even found myself telling Ingrid the circumstances of Oliver's death. Which is an event whose details I very rarely confide to anyone, certainly not on a first meeting. But – as I'm sure many people had done before – I felt real empathy with Ingrid Richards.

Then we got on to her work, and what she was currently doing.

'I get asked occasionally to comment on some new disaster in the Middle East. Television sometimes, more often in print these days. Back where I started, writing copy, as a cub reporter on the *Liverpool Daily Echo* . . . which no longer exists, like so many regional newspapers. But I can still meet a deadline and, unlike most so-called journalists these days, I have actually been to the places I write about. I don't do it all from behind a keyboard in an office in Wapping.'

Her voice carried a heavy load of contempt for the current state of the Press. 'And then of course,' she went on, 'there's the *magnum opus.*'

'What's that?'

'I'm writing a memoir of my life.'

'Warts and all?'

'Most of the warts I encountered are now dead.' She chuckled at her little joke. 'But yes, it'll cover the whole gamut – professional and personal.'

'Is it commissioned?' I asked, knowing a bit about such matters from Oliver's dealings with publishers.

'Of course it bloody is!' she snapped, angry for the first time. 'I'm a professional. I stopped doing stuff on spec in the 1970s. And all this' – she gestured to the piles of papers and notebooks on her desk – 'is taking me back to those places where I worked. I've spent the last two weeks trying to remind myself of all the militia groups there were in Beirut during the hostage crisis. God, it was so complicated. I had a handle on it at the time but wow, trying to put together all the details now in a way which the average reader's going to understand . . . my brain hurts.

'You'd think a civil war would be between two sides, wouldn't you? And maybe the Lebanese one started off that way, basically Maronite forces against the Palestinian Liberation Organization, but in Lebanon nothing is that simple. You've got conflict between Sunnis and Shias, Christians and Muslims. Then Syria and Israel get involved, while all the time strings are being pulled by the Ayatollahs in Iran and Reagan in the States.

'Of course, in the Middle East, hostage-taking has always been a popular political pastime, and suddenly the militias think there might be mileage in capturing a few foreigners. They start with Americans, obviously, but that soon spreads to other nationalities. And in the slums of south Beirut you've got poor buggers chained to radiators in God knows how many basements. And some seriously stupid things happen – particularly when that idiot, that sententious scoutmaster Terry Waite parades himself asking to be captured and . . .'

She stopped herself and looked at me with a crooked grin. 'Sorry. You didn't come here for a history lesson, did you, Ellen?'

'No.'

'It just all comes back to me so vividly. It was completely lawless on the streets of Beirut. Thing that stays with me is that you were always walking on broken glass. Never forget that sound of crunching underfoot. Everywhere you went, there had just been some atrocity. Mind you, the lawlessness on the streets was matched by the lawlessness in the place where the foreign correspondents hung out. The Commodore Hotel, of course, just near the Hamra shopping centre. And then some people liked to drink in the Pickwick Bar at the Mayflower Hotel. God, that was a bizarre place, an English country pub with imported keg beer, stuck in the middle of Beirut. Run by that former Spitfire pilot Jackie Mann, who, later, of course, in 1989, became a hostage himself and was held for two years in . . .'

Again, she curbed her tongue. 'Sorry. From the glaze in your eyes, Ellen, I detect that I need to work harder to make my account riveting to the average reader.'

'I apologize,' I said.

'Don't worry about it. Sad fact of life – or perhaps actually a rather encouraging fact of life – one cannot simulate interest in something that doesn't interest one.'

'No,' I said honestly. 'I'm afraid not. I have to confess, if I were reading the book, I'd be much more interested in the personal than the professional side of your life.'

'Ah. Maybe that's a gender thing.'

'I don't know. Do you think it is?'

'Yes. It's like women enjoy reading romances, because they actually *care* who ends up with who. Men don't give a shit.'

'Easier being a man, do you think?'

'Not sure. I just know I never wanted to be one. All that tedious conversation you have to have with other men, talking about football and Formula One, rather than saying what you're really feeling. God, it must be boring. I've loved being a woman.'

'Me too.'

There was a silence. We both sipped our Jameson's. Then Ingrid said, 'You'll still have to buy a copy of my memoir when it comes out, Ellen. You can skip the political bits. I promise you there'll be plenty of personal stuff to keep you interested.'

'I look forward to it.'

'Oh yes,' said Ingrid Richards, a roguish smile developing around her lips. 'When the memoir's published, it won't only be from my cupboard that the skeletons come rattling out!'

SEVEN

A s we lifted it down from the back of his van, Dodge looked at the piece of furniture doubtfully. It was one of those old-fashioned cupboards designed to contain a television, back in the days when people didn't like to have their screens vulgarly on display but, at non-viewing times, kept them shut away in genteel invisibility.

Dodge's was not the doubtful look of a junk merchant, about to say that nobody wanted to buy stuff like that these days. It was the doubtful look of an avid recycler, who just hadn't yet worked out what he was going to turn the piece into. But who would soon come up with an idea. With Dodge, nothing was wasted.

The piece was maybe four foot high. Beneath the double doors, which hid the offensive screen, were a row of four narrow drawers. The whole thing was veneered in light oak, not in bad condition but just desperately old-fashioned. It had belonged to Minnie, one of the many people whose hoarding habit had started following the death of a spouse. Brought in by the social services, I had helped her tackle the problem and she, like a good few of my elderly clients, had become one of those on whom I still kept an eye. A visit every week or so, for which she was always excessively grateful. Another whose underlying problem was loneliness.

Minnie had been a London tour guide and retained an insatiable curiosity about the capital's history. The clutter had started with her buying too many books on the subject and then, when her husband died, it had escalated into the accumulation of all kinds of stuff she was incapable of throwing away.

Having spent her entire professional life talking to people about London, it remained the basis of her conversation, and I would always leave our decluttering sessions full of new information. For instance, she'd tell me that a 'Desmond' was

a 'jacket', Cockney Rhyming Slang based on the name of
Desmond Hackett, a *Daily Express* football reporter from the
1950s. Or that the place name 'Ealing' derived from
the seventh-century Old English 'Gillingas', meaning 'the
settlement of Gilla's family'. Amazing, the stuff you learn as
a declutterer.

A recent stroke, however, had made it impossible for Minnie
to continue living on her own and condemned her to one of
the local authority's care homes. That meant emptying her
house for sale to contribute to the costs. I don't normally do
basic clearance, but Minnie was so anxious about what was
going to happen to her precious possessions that I said I would
find good homes for them. And there couldn't be a better home
for anything than with Dodge.

'Do you fancy a cup of tea?'

I did. I felt better than I had any right to after the amount
of Jameson's I'd put away the night before. But a cup of
Dodge's nettle tea would be just the thing to ease my residual
dehydration. I followed him through into his living quarters.

Dodge lived outside the village of Walberton, near
Arundel, in what I think must once have been a farm, all
of whose fields had been sold off for development. (There
are a lot of properties like that in West Sussex.) The main
house he used for the meticulous storage of all the materials
he would use in his recycling. Then there were two substantial outbuildings with corrugated-iron roofs. One was his
workshop, the other where he lived and slept, in conditions
of enviable minimalism.

It was there that he put a battered kettle on the salvaged
cast-iron range to make the nettle tea. Normally the space only
contained Dodge's bed and a table with one chair, so I was
surprised to see more furniture there. A couple of cupboards,
a child's desk and chair. I was about to comment, then realized
that he probably moved completed pieces away from the dust
and paint spills of his workshop.

I looked more closely at them. As ever, perfectly finished.
I had given up trying to guess what Dodge's furniture had
been in its former life, his craft was so meticulous.

'Lovely stuff,' I commented.

'They're for Mary Griffin,' he confided awkwardly. 'Well, that is, for her little girl. I'm going to put on more *Frozen* stickers.'

'Amy'll love them,' I said. 'She and Mary'll be over the moon.'

'I feel very protective towards them,' said Dodge. 'Mary and Amy.'

Which was, when I thought about it, rather a strange thing for him to say.

Then it was back to the bloody invoices, whose processing had been interrupted when I'd realized the previous evening that I was nearly going to be late for Ingrid Richards. The mobile rang as soon as I started on them (having made do with toasted cheese by way of lunch). The display said: 'Fleur'. I connected, as ever, with a slight feeling of foreboding.

'Ellen dahling . . . just ringing for a little chatette . . .' She knew full well how much her using words like that irritated me.

'Maybe I could call you back this evening, Fleur . . .? I am working and I—'

As ever, she steamrolled her way through this. She'd never regarded my work as important. 'I was just wondering, dahling, whether you'd heard anything from my chum Jools recently . . .?'

'No,' I replied through gritted teeth. Though perhaps 'chum' was better than the other word she often used, 'girlfriend'.

'I thought you might not have done,' said Fleur, as ever digging away. 'Anyway, she's made me a very generous offer. You know she's got that lovely flat in Herne Hill . . .?'

Of course, I bloody did. If I hadn't stumped up the deposit, she wouldn't have been able to buy it. But I said nothing.

'And you know, dahling, that I'm really a London person . . .'

She kept saying this, even though her husband Kenneth, the solicitor who funded her extravagant lifestyle, was firmly based in Chichester.

'You know, I *bloom* in London. I feel *refreshed* by the polluted air. Just wandering through the West End *energizes* me. I love revisiting the scenes of my former triumphs. All those First Nights, all those backstage memories . . . And the bars and the cafés and the restaurants and the shops . . . Scenes of so many liaisons . . . London is just *me!*'

I still didn't say anything, waiting to see where all this was leading.

'Anyway, dahling Jools . . . my *girlfriend* Jools' – I knew it would come – '*understands* me.' With the unspoken implication that I didn't. 'She's a London creature too . . . and realizes how much my soul is *nourished* just by being in the place . . . and Jools knows how disappointed I feel when I have to curtail my metropolitan delights by needing to catch the last train back to dreary old Chichester . . . and so she – the little angel – has said that, whenever I want to . . . there's a spare bed I can use in her bijou little flatette!'

'Well, that'll be very nice for you,' I said, somewhat drily.

'I assume Jools has made the same offer to you,' insinuated Fleur, knowing that she hadn't.

Maybe it was talking about the child with whom I didn't have a relaxed relationship made me think about the one with whom I did. Or at least I always had had in the past. Though now I wondered. Insecurity about Ben was niggling away at me.

I don't know if it was a gender thing, but I'd always felt closer to him than Jools. As a little child, she had always been a 'Daddy's girl', but drifted away from Oliver in the year before he died. And when he did die, she seemed almost indifferent to his absence. I knew she couldn't really be, but she had found a very efficient way of damming up her emotions and, coincidentally, shutting me out. I sometimes worried what would happen when the floodgates opened. Currently, though, her self-constructed dam showed no signs of fracture.

I knew it was too soon after my last attempt to contact Ben. I didn't want to sound like a worried mother. Tough, of course, because that was exactly what I was. I rang the mobile and got his voicemail again. Of course I did. He was a student, it was term-time, he was in a lecture or a seminar or at the library. I left no message. I stopped the call.

But I couldn't leave it there. Instead, I texted him. The minimum. 'All OK? Love, Mum.'

The moment I'd sent it, I felt stupid and overreacting. I returned sheepishly to the invoices.

Almost as quickly as he could possibly have done it, my mobile pinged with his returned text.

'Take a chill pill, Ma. No red hair issues. X B.'

It made me smile. When Ben called me 'Ma', it was always in a slightly joshing manner, as though he had put the word in quotes. The use of 'chill pill' was also slightly sending me up. He had a habit of addressing me in old-fashioned slang.

The 'red hair' was also reassuring. And it did answer the question I'd really been wanting to ask him. Ben was quoting his father. I don't think Oliver had ever used the expression directly to him, but he'd said it often enough to me and I must have passed it on to Ben.

It concerned the depression that father and son shared. There are many theories of what causes the illness. It can be triggered by a trauma like bereavement or abuse. It can hit someone suddenly in the middle of their adult life. For others, their entire lives have been bedevilled by low moods.

Oliver was in the latter category. He couldn't remember a time when he hadn't suffered from depression. As he often told me, 'It's genetic. It's like having red hair.'

Ben knew his shorthand would have reassured me. But I wished he'd called rather than texted. I really wanted to hear his voice. I wanted him to tell me about Tracey.

These bloody invoices are never going to get finished, I thought, as the mobile rang again. The hope that it might be Ben, having changed his mind about talking, was quickly dashed.

'Good afternoon, Ellen. This is Cara.'

'Hello.' I didn't sound encouraging. I'd got the feeling the day before that Cara Reece was a talker who I didn't want to get too involved with. She may have been instrumental in making Edward Finch contact me, but he was the client, not her.

'I just thought I should give you some background to Eddie's situation,' she said.

'Oh? Why?'

'Because he does sometimes say some strange things about Pauline and how she died.'

I'd already experienced the 'strange things' but, of course, Cara didn't know that. 'What kind of things?' I asked warily.

'The fact is that she died in the bath. She drowned.'

'Was there a post-mortem?'

'Yes. She was found to have had a heart attack.'

'So that killed her rather than the drowning?'

'I don't know. I didn't see the documentation for the post-mortem, so I couldn't be sure of that. It wouldn't be regarded as my business, would it?'

'No,' I agreed, trying to invest the monosyllable with the implication that her contacting me again about Edward was not really her business either.

My deterring tactic didn't work because she went on, 'Eddie told me, though, that Pauline had a heart attack because she thought she was about to be drowned. It was fear that triggered it. Because he had said he was going to drown her.'

'And do you think that's true, Cara?'

'If it isn't true, why would he tell me that's what happened?'

'There was no investigation from the police? They didn't suspect foul play had been involved?'

'I don't know about that.'

'Hm,' I said. 'Well, look, I've arranged to go and see Edward tomorrow. I'm not going to change my plans. If he tells me that he drowned his wife in the bath, I may feel differently.'

'Thank you,' said Cara. 'It is rather worrying, isn't it?'

'How long had you known the Finches?'

'Oh, a long time. We all taught at the same school. And all retired round the same time.'

'And would you say Edward and Pauline's was a happy marriage?'

'Outwardly,' Cara replied. And she relished the note of mystery that she put into the word.

I don't always watch the television local news in the morning, but I had it on in the kitchen as I was getting my breakfast together on the Wednesday.

There was a report of a fire that had gutted a top-floor flat in Brunswick Square in Hove. One person was believed to have died.

They didn't say it was Ingrid Richards' flat. Perhaps the identity of the owner had not yet been confirmed.

But I kind of knew.

EIGHT

'**M**eek' was the word. Meek was how I would describe Edward Finch, particularly on second acquaintance. The idea of him as a murderer was totally incongruous.

He certainly didn't mention it again and I wasn't about to raise the subject. Even with the further detail provided by Cara Reece, I still didn't believe his claim. But I was intrigued to find out why he had made it. The psychological effects of bereavement I find endlessly fascinating. And I thought, spending time with Edward sorting out his practical problem might enable me to find out what made him tick psychologically.

But working with him that morning I have to confess he didn't have my full attention. Part of my mind was in Brunswick Square, waiting for the inevitable confirmation of the fire victim's name.

I didn't take anything from the Yeti into the bungalow with me when I arrived that morning. I hoped by the end of the session to be leaving with some of Pauline Finch's clothes to take to a charity shop, but I didn't want her widower to feel threatened by my coming in loaded with boxes and bin bags. Talk first, then action.

I suggested moving the boxes from the hall and he did not object. Indeed, he helped me fill the Yeti's boot with them. It was just general household rubbish, destined for the dump. The hall was clear within ten minutes and then he offered me a coffee.

Edward went through the same ritual of making the drinks in the kitchen and we sat down in the sitting room to drink them. Someone – he, Cara? – had actually made an attempt at tidying there. The scattered books on the floor had been straightened up into piles. The magazines and the out-of-date newspapers had been removed. As I had thought on my previous visit, most of the bungalow's rooms just needed a brisk tidy-up. It was in the bedroom at the back that the real problem lay.

I started by checking some of the basics. 'Edward, how long ago is it that Pauline died?' I always prefer the words 'die' and 'death' to any of the popular euphemisms. 'Passed', 'passed away' are just attempts to sanitize the reality.

'Ten months,' he replied.

'And did you stop sleeping in the back bedroom immediately?'

'Yes. There were too many memories. I couldn't . . .' He couldn't finish the sentence, apart from anything else.

'I fully understand.' I didn't spell out how fully by mentioning Oliver's death. It wasn't appropriate. My grief was my own, not to be shared with strangers. If I got into a deeper relationship with a client, I might talk about it. Sometimes that had proved helpful in cases of bereavement. But my dealings with Edward Finch were at a very early stage.

'And when,' I went on, 'did you put her clothes all over the bedroom?'

'That's relatively recent,' he said. 'The last couple of months, I suppose. It was the first time I'd been in there since . . . since . . .'

'But it was quite clean,' I said.

'What do you mean?'

'When you showed me the room on Monday, yes, it was covered with clothes. But it wasn't as dusty or cobwebby as a space would be if it hadn't been entered for eight months.'

'No.'

'Did you sweep it up, hoover it?'

'No.'

'Who did then?'

'Cara.'

'Ah. Cara did actually ring me, after I'd come here on Monday.'

'I know. She told me.'

'She told me that all three of you, Pauline as well, taught at the same school.'

'Yes, we did.'

'Cara clearly helps you a lot.'

'You could call it helping,' he said rather petulantly. 'You could call it interfering, not minding her own business.'

I didn't comment. I thought Edward Finch was being ungrateful to someone who clearly had his welfare at heart, but I wasn't about to take sides in what was probably a long-running disagreement.

'What you're experiencing, Edward,' I said gently, 'is something that is quite a common reaction in cases of bereavement. Lots of people find it exceedingly difficult to clear up the dead person's belongings. Doing that has such an air of finality about it. It can be like finally admitting to yourself that they're really never coming back. Was that how it felt to you?'

'Maybe. A bit,' he mumbled.

'And you've only tried clearing up Pauline's stuff on your own?'

'How else should I do it?' he almost snapped.

'With someone else to help you. I thought Cara might have—'

'Cara did suggest that she should help me. Typical, yet again muscling in on our lives.'

The use of 'our' was interesting. And, again, very common. Many of the bereaved find it takes a long time to take on board that their plural lives have become singular. Even though it's more than eight years since Oliver died, I still sometimes find myself slipping into the 'we' usage.

'Well, look, Edward, what I'm suggesting is that I should go to the bedroom with you and see if the two of us can impose some order on the chaos. Or would you regard that as me "muscling in"?'

'No. We could try.'

'We'll take it at your pace. I'm not going to rush you into doing anything you don't want to do.'

'Right. Thank you.' He swallowed down the last of his coffee. 'I'm prepared to give it a go.' He rose to his feet. 'So, what – we put everything back in the wardrobe and the drawers?'

I shook my head. 'I'm sorry, Edward. That'd just be kicking the can further down the road.'

'How do you mean?'

'Pauline's clothes will still be in the bedroom. It'd be just as if you'd never even started to move them.'

'So . . . where are you suggesting we put them? This bungalow doesn't have a cellar or an attic. Or a garage, come to that. And the garden shed would be far too damp. The clothes'd get ruined in there.'

'Edward, this may sound very cruel to you, but what I'm suggesting is that we move them out of the house.'

'How?' He responded as if I'd suggested moving the Tower of London. The idea was incongruous to him. It was a feat beyond his imagination.

'We'll do it gradually,' I said. 'I'll get some boxes and we'll put some of the stuff in them.'

'And then what? Burn the clothes? Send them to landfill?'

'I'd rather not do either of those things. I can see there's some lovely stuff there. Hardly worn, a lot of it. Some of it might have resale value.' I made that sound unlikely. Second-hand clothes had to be a lot older and more individual to be of interest to the vintage retailers.

'I'm not looking to make money out of my dead wife,' said Edward Finch, almost insulted.

'No, that wasn't what I was suggesting,' I quickly assured him. 'Of course, it's your decision, Edward, but my solution would be to take the best of the clothes, the stuff that's still wearable, to a charity shop and then someone else could benefit from wearing them.'

'What?' He didn't like the idea. 'So, I might be walking round Lancing one morning and see other women wearing Pauline's clothes?'

'No, I wouldn't take it to a charity shop on your doorstep. And a lot of the garments, I could see, were high-street brands. Other women will have bought the same styles as Pauline did, so you'd see them anyway.'

'I don't know,' said Edward Finch anxiously.

'Let's give it a try,' I said.

I was there a couple of hours that morning and achieved a modest level of success. Progress was slow. Each of his dead wife's garments prompted some memory, where and when it had been bought, the events she had worn it to. But I'm used to hearing that stuff and I respect it. The past is important to people and I would never deny anyone the right to their own reminiscences.

By twelve o'clock, we'd got two cardboard boxes full of clothes out of the bedroom and into the hall. And when I say 'we', I mean it. I consulted Edward Finch on every item before he agreed that it should be transferred.

There was still a lot scattered over the bedroom, but I felt we'd made a meaningful start. The Yeti boot was full of the stuff from the hall. I was tied up with other clients the next day, but I proposed coming back the same time on the Friday morning to take the boxes of Pauline's clothes.

He was agreeable to that. He seemed more relaxed than he had when I'd arrived. Perhaps actually starting to move his wife's possessions made him realize that, though a painful process, it was achievable.

We were making progress.

In the car on the way back to Chichester, I heard the one o'clock news. The body found in the burnt-out flat in Brunswick Square Hove had been identified as that of the legendary war reporter, Ingrid Richards.

NINE

The Thursday was kind of an average working day for me – no clients I had not had previous contact with, just continuing support for the existing ones. Which is what I spend a lot of my time doing.

First, I paid another visit to Mary Griffin. I could have asked her on the phone, but I wanted to see for myself how she'd progressed with turning her devastated house back into a home. And, more importantly, how Amy had reacted to her changed environment.

Somewhat to my surprise, as I parked the Yeti, I saw a familiar 1951 Morris Commercial CV9/40 Tipper outside the house. When Mary led me into the kitchen (which now looked like a kitchen), I found Dodge there with a cup of coffee. He didn't look relaxed – I've only ever seen him look relaxed when deeply involved in his construction work – and he didn't make eye contact with either Mary or me, but I was intrigued by his presence there.

Surely there couldn't be any romantic interest between him and Mary . . .? I had gleaned over the years I'd known him that the breakdown which turned Gervaise the consumerist City whiz kid into Dodge the recycler had also involved the ending of a relationship. And, though he'd never said as much, I'm fairly sure that relationship had been with a woman. At what level, though, whether they had been married or cohabiting, I hadn't found out. And it wasn't my business. I never pushed Dodge for information about his past. Anything I did know was stuff he had volunteered. Sometimes reluctantly. Like the fact that he helped out young people in a drug rehabilitation programme. He'd also implied that drugs might have been a contributory cause of his breakdown.

But, since I'd known him, he'd never shown signs of sexual interest in anyone.

And it was clear that nothing of that kind was needed to

explain his presence in Mary Griffin's kitchen when I was taken upstairs to meet Amy.

She was an enchanting little girl with her mother's brown eyes. But Amy's looked unclouded by fear. Whatever scenes she may have witnessed in that house, she appeared untraumatized by the experience. That might be different if she woke from a bad dream in the night, but at that moment she irradiated the whole room with her happiness. And I could see how much that was helping her mother's healing process.

The immediate reason for her joy was in front of her. She sat on a little Amy-sized pink wooden chair, in front of a pink-painted Amy-sized dressing table. There were four drawers down one side with a smooth wooden top running across to two stout legs the other side. Leaving a perfect Amy's-knee-sized space for her to sit in comfort at the dressing table. On the surface in front of her stood an adjustable mirror. Its frame and the front of the drawers were decorated with *Frozen* stickers.

I was surprised by a sudden pang of memory, of a time when I was pregnant with Ben. Juliet at the same age as Amy, before she became the distant Jools, reacting with ecstasy to a picture of ballet dancers (her then obsession) that Oliver had painted for her third birthday. I wondered if she still had it. Or had she excised the painting from her life, as she had everything else that might remind her of her father? The recollection of Curtis family happiness was sharply painful.

Back in the present, as ever, Dodge's eyes would not meet those of the three females in the room, but he knew how gratefully his skills had been appreciated.

It was only then that I realized that the set of drawers which formed the structural basis for Amy's dressing table had once sat underneath the doors of a genteel television-disguiser.

So, it was appropriate that my next visit that morning was to see Minnie in her care home. It's a local authority one and only just the right side of adequate. The old girl hadn't fully recovered her speech after the stroke which put a stop to her independent life. I could understand her slurred sentences because I'd worked at deciphering them, but I doubted whether any of the overworked care-home staff had had time to put in that kind of effort. A lot of them didn't have English as a first language, so sometimes it was difficult for Minnie to understand them as well. And most of the other residents were too demented to hold a sensible conversation, anyway.

I never asked, but I have a horrible feeling I was Minnie's only visitor. In spite of her disability, though, she could still read and more-or-less write. So, she kept up her endless search for more information about London. And I worked hard to decipher the nuggets of information she passed on to me. For instance, I left the care home that day, knowing that meat sold at the February 1814 Frost Fair on the frozen Thames, at the extortionate price of a shilling a slice, was known as 'Lapland mutton'.

For lunch I got a tuna and cucumber sandwich to eat in the Yeti and while I was in the Co-op bought a copy of the *Guardian*. Though I get the *Observer* delivered at the weekend, I only buy a daily when I know I'm going to have time to read it. There are many days when work takes over and all I'm capable of when I get home is getting something basic to eat and slumping with a glass of Merlot in front of some mindless medical soap opera.

The *Guardian*'s front page was dominated by Ingrid Richards. A huge photograph – red hair blazing, the defiant dent of the shrapnel wound in her forehead – and tributes from famous friends and admirers – relegated all the latest international disasters and idiocies of government to second-feature status. The obituary inside spread over more than one page.

I remembered Oliver's assertion that journalists thought they were far more important than they actually were, but the list of Ingrid Richards' achievements justified the space she was allotted.

I was amazed at how many wars she had covered. That tall red-haired figure with a microphone reporting from a vista of shattered concrete had become so familiar on the television screen that one almost forgot that they were all different theatres of destruction. Kosovo, Chechnya, Afghanistan, Palestine, East Timor, Libya, Syria, Yemen . . . wherever the inhumanity of war was on display, Ingrid Richards had been there. Usually in body armour, with the strap of a leather satchel diagonally across her front.

I also found in the *Guardian* obituary more detail about the scar on her forehead. My basic recollection of what had happened proved to be accurate. The wound had been caused by shrapnel. Ingrid had been in Beirut in 1986, reporting on the hostage crisis, along with a BBC cameraman called Phil Dickie. They'd been filming a report when a car bomb went off only yards from where they were standing. Dickie, who'd been nearer the vehicle, had been much the more seriously injured and, in fact, his body had shielded Ingrid from the blast. But she had taken a lot of shrapnel, including the piece that had given her the trademark scar. Both she and the cameraman had survived the blast and been flown back to the UK for some months of hospitalization.

Reading the account in the obituary, I remembered coverage of the incident at the time, when I was in my early twenties. And I remembered the debate it prompted as to whether female reporters should be allowed to place themselves in danger on the front line. It would be taken for granted now, so maybe there have been some advances in gender equality. Not as many as I would wish for, though. And, coward that I am, the right to put myself in the way of bomb blasts is one that I would happily forgo.

I checked online for obituaries in the other dailies. They were all full of praise for an exceptional woman, who had repeatedly demonstrated unrivalled bravery without losing her humanity and vulnerability. It was universally thought to be a tragedy that the life of such an icon should be ended by a domestic accident.

The obituaries did not evade the fact that Ingrid Richards' private life had also been a battleground. There were the two short-lived marriages. As she'd said to me, they 'didn't take'. Alexandra was mentioned fleetingly, but not the name of her father. Which I thought was slightly strange. Ingrid had told me there was no secret about it. The information was even available on Wikipedia. Maybe in the obituaries Niall Connor had been protected from being named by some old-fashioned Fleet Street *omertà*.

Reading so much about her, I felt honoured to have met Ingrid Richards, albeit so late in her life.

But I couldn't get out of my mind a few sentences she had spoken during our bonding over the Jameson's. 'I'm extremely careful about my personal safety. My experience of war zones has taught me how to avoid avoidable risks. There are no doubt people out there who'd like to kill me – I've rubbed a lot of people up the wrong way in the course of my career – but there's no way I'll die by accident.'

Two o'clock I was due at Edward Finch's. I arrived in Lancing early, as I always like to for an appointment, and parked round the corner from his bungalow to check the mobile. I'd heard the ping of an incoming call on the way over. I do have the facility for hands-free calls, but I find they distract me from driving, so I rarely answer until I'm parked up. Unless, of course, it's Ben calling.

A woman's voice had left a message asking me to call back. It was only when I got through to her that she identified herself as a police officer. A Detective Sergeant Unwin. Sounded bossy, which I guess is an occupational hazard – or indeed an essential qualification. She asked first whether I had heard the news of Ingrid Richards' death. I assured her I had.

'We've spoken to the deceased's daughter and she said that her mother had engaged your professional services.'

'That's not strictly accurate, Sergeant,' I said. 'I only had the one exploratory meeting with her. It was Alexandra herself, not Ingrid, who contacted me. She was worried about her mother's situation.'

'What situation would that be, Mrs Curtis?'

'The safety of her lifestyle.'

'Sorry? What is it exactly that you do, Mrs Curtis?'

'I declutter. I help people organize their possessions when they get out of hand.'

'Oh. Is that a job?'

'Yes, it is,' I said, sharply. I had heard the question too often not to be defensive about what I do.

'And you had taken on that job for the deceased?'

'I hadn't, no. As I said, my meeting with her on Monday

was just a preliminary discussion, to see whether Alexandra was right, whether her mother did actually need my services.'

'What conclusion did you reach?'

'That Ingrid Richards did not need my services.'

'Thank you, Mrs Curtis. Obviously, the reason I'm asking you these questions is because we are investigating the cause of Ingrid Richards' death. So, are you telling me that her flat in Brunswick Square was not a fire hazard?'

'I'm not telling you that, Sergeant, no. I think, for someone less organized than Ingrid Richards, it could have been a fire hazard.'

'Surely something's a fire hazard or it isn't?' There was the bossy tone again. 'As Alexandra Richards described it to us, her mother's flat was full of old newspapers and magazines. Is that not true?'

'It is true, but—'

'Alexandra Richards also said that her mother was virtually a chain-smoker and a very heavy drinker. Are those facts not true either?'

'No, they're true. And, as I said, someone else in those circumstances might have been a danger to herself and others. But I got the impression that Ingrid Richards was very much in control of the way she lived.'

'What gave you that impression, Mrs Curtis?'

'She told me she was.'

That made Detective Sergeant Unwin chuckle. 'Yeah, but old people are like that. They never realize when they're losing it. Take my mother-in-law and her driving. She's nearly ninety, she thinks she's still safe on the roads, but she's a bloody liability.'

This was more information than I required. I had no interest in the woman's mother-in-law.

'Listen, Mrs Curtis,' she went on before I could say anything, 'Alexandra Richards suggested we should contact you because you had recently inspected the Brunswick Square property . . .'

'Hardly "inspected". I just went for a chat with—'

'But, in the course of your work, Mrs Curtis, you must see the homes of many people with hoarding problems.'

'Of course I do.'

'And, in some cases, you must see situations where the hoarding has created fire hazards?'

'I certainly have.'

'So, in your professional capacity, you would very definitely recognize a fire hazard when you saw one?'

'Yes.'

'All I need from you, Mrs Curtis, is confirmation of what we were told by the deceased's daughter, Alexandra Richards, that her mother's flat was a fire hazard.'

'Well . . .'

'Was it, Mrs Curtis?'

It was too difficult to explain Ingrid Richards' mature awareness of the risk and her resolution not to succumb to it.

'Yes, Sergeant,' I said wretchedly.

When he opened the door to me, there was something both smug and shameful in Edward Finch's manner. He was like a little boy who knew he had been naughty but was rather proud of his naughtiness.

I soon realized what had happened. The cardboard boxes I had so carefully packed with his dead wife's clothes two days before were no longer in the hall. No, that's not quite accurate. The boxes *were* there in the hall, but they had had the tape holding them in shape cut through. They were once again flattened, just as I carried them in the Yeti. And of their contents there was no sign.

Wordlessly, Edward led me through the door at the end of the hall that opened on to the master bedroom. The clothes had been draped back over the bed and floor, exactly as they had been before I collected them up and packed them.

'I'm sorry, Ellen,' he said. 'I just couldn't do it.'

TEN

I t would have been different if Edward Finch had been referred to me by the social services. Then I would have felt I had to sort out his problem. But he'd contacted me off his own bat. He'd asked for my advice; I'd given it and he had chosen to disregard it.

I didn't think his situation was worse than that of any other bereaved husband. And he had the advantage of the devoted Cara to help him out. However much he disparaged what she did for him, she ensured that his living conditions didn't descend into total squalor.

So, I told Edward Finch that unless he was prepared to change his attitude, I couldn't help him any more. If he decided he could change, then he should contact me again.

I also said that I would invoice him for the two visits I'd made after the initial consultation. I hadn't got time to waste with habitual time-wasters.

'Do you fancy another meeting on the beach at Littlehampton?' Alexandra's voice sounded unaccountably cheerful, even jaunty.

'Well, yes. That'd be fine.' By the Friday, I was desperate to talk to someone about the death of Ingrid Richards, but there had really been no reason for me to contact her daughter. Except maybe to offer condolences. So, I was glad that Alexandra had rung me.

'Even better,' she said, 'why don't I buy you lunch at that nice East Beach Café?'

The lunch was very good. Given the location, it was no surprise that the menu featured a lot of seafood. Excellent seafood, imaginatively cooked.

Alexandra was keen on the idea of sharing a bottle of white wine and disappointed when I said no. I don't drink at lunchtime during the week. Preservation of my driving licence again. And preservation of the focus I need for work. Alexandra suggested that I should just have one glass, but again I said no. If I had one, I'd want another. In such circumstances, I always find it easier not to drink at all. Sorry if that sounds priggish.

'So,' I suggested, 'I'll raise a glass of sparkling mineral water to Ingrid's memory.'

'Fine,' she said, a little grudgingly as she ordered it, along with a glass of Pinot Grigio for herself.

'I am, incidentally, Alexandra, very sorry about your mother's death.'

'Oh yes. Thank you.' She didn't sound interested in my condolences. 'So far as I'm concerned, it's just a huge relief.'

The force with which this was said made me wonder whether Alexandra had already had a drink that morning. Though it's a common instinctive reaction, there is still an atavistic taboo about admitting one is pleased by the death of a family member.

She seemed to remember that and attempted a cover-up by saying, 'All I mean is that I'm glad Ingrid went while she was still more or less in control of her faculties. She would have loathed the gradual degeneration of age, hated not being able to do the things she enjoyed doing. The thought of Ingrid in a care home . . . well, it doesn't bear thinking of. She always said she wanted a quick sudden death that she knew nothing about.'

I wondered how closely being incinerated in a top-floor flat fitted that definition, but I didn't say anything, as Alexandra went on, 'Ingrid would have hated losing control.'

'Wouldn't you say,' I suggested, 'that allowing her flat to burn down from what . . . an inadequately stubbed-out Gauloise . . . meant that she was already losing control?'

'Perhaps.' The drinks arrived. Alexandra immediately took a long swallow from hers. I didn't think it'd be the only one she had over lunch.

Then she said, 'Of course, because of the way things happened, you never did report back to me about whether you thought Ingrid needed your decluttering services.'

'Sorry. I was busy the next day and—'

'No worries. I think we left it that I was going to ring you, anyway.' She took another substantial swallow of Pinot Grigio. 'She liked you, you know.'

'What?'

'Ingrid. She really liked you. When you went to see her. And she wasn't a woman to take an instant liking to everyone, so that's quite an accolade.'

'I'm suitably honoured.' And I was. I had been instantly at ease with Ingrid Richards, but I wasn't convinced until then that the feeling had been mutual.

'What, incidentally, Ellen, was your professional view?'

'As to whether your mother needed the services of a declutterer?'

'Yes.'

'Right. My professional view was that, had I been inspecting the premises of anyone of that age other than Ingrid, I would have recommended some tidying up for safety reasons. With your mother, though, I thought she was more than capable of looking after herself. I would not have advised taking any decluttering action.'

'Hm.' Alexandra grinned wryly. 'Well, you were wrong, weren't you? As it turned out.'

I hadn't really thought of that before. But I suppose, by any objective analysis, she was right.

The waitress arrived to take our order. Before food was mentioned, Alexandra swallowed down the remains of her Pinot Grigio and asked for another.

We both went for fish and chips. Dodgy choice in some pubs in the area, where you get presented with a strip of battered cardboard. But I knew they did them very well at the East Beach Café.

'So,' I said, 'you spoke to Ingrid after my visit?'

'Yes. On Tuesday. God, that seems an age ago now.'

'Tuesday? The day she died?'

'That's right. Well, I haven't heard what time the fire was reckoned to have happened. I supposed she could have died on the Wednesday morning.'

'But you rang her on the Tuesday?'

'Better than that. I went to see her on the Tuesday. Dutiful daughter or what?'

I couldn't stop myself from asking, 'What time of day did you see her?'

Fortunately, Alexandra didn't notice that this question belonged more in the category of interrogation than casual enquiry. I still wasn't convinced Ingrid Richards' death had been an accident and was hungry for any information I could get about her last hours.

'Early evening,' she replied. 'Round six thirty, I suppose.'

'And did she behave unusually in any way?'

'What do you mean?'

'Well, did she say anything that was unexpected?'

'Sorry?' Her second Pinot Grigio arrived. She took a healthy swallow from it. I wondered if this was a taste she'd inherited from her mother. Alexandra grinned with sudden realization. 'Oh, I see. You're asking if she said anything about wanting to top herself?'

That wasn't what I'd been asking. The thought hadn't occurred to me. And I'm extremely sensitive on the subject of suicide.

'No,' I replied. 'I just wondered if she'd talked about . . . I don't know . . . other visitors she was expecting that evening . . .?'

I'd tried to make the question sound disingenuous, but it prompted a sharp look of suspicion. 'No, she didn't,' Alexandra said firmly. 'Incidentally, Ellen, have the police been on to you?'

I couldn't deny it. I had no reason to deny it.

'I hope you didn't mind.'

'Mind? Why should I mind?'

'They asked me about people who'd visited Ingrid recently and I mentioned you.'

'Not a problem. Telling the truth to the police can often save you a lot of trouble.'

'Mm. And when they heard why you'd visited her, they were keen to get your views on, you know, how safe she was in the flat?'

'Yes. That's what the detective sergeant asked me about.'

I realized she must have given me her name, but I couldn't remember it.

Alexandra took another long swallow of Pinot Grigio. When she resumed, there was a new note in her voice, as if she was fishing for something. 'He didn't say anything else, did he?'

'She. It was a woman.'

'Ah. It was only men who talked to me.'

'Probably quite a big team on an investigation like that.'

'Yes.' Again, the wheedling note. 'So, did this detective sergeant ask about anything else?'

'No. Why should she?'

'I don't know. I was just wondering whether she gave any indication of what they thought had happened . . . you know, with Ingrid . . .?'

'I'm sure, if the police had reached any conclusions on the subject, they wouldn't be about to share them with me, would they?'

'No. No, probably not.' Another slurp of wine. Then, 'Did she actually use the word "accident"?'

'Not so far as I recall.' I took a sip of mineral water. 'Why? Is there some thought it might not have been an accident?'

'No,' she said quickly. Too quickly? She certainly seemed keen to change the subject. 'Do you mind if I put someone else in touch with you?'

'Someone else with a hoarding problem?'

'No. This is still about Ingrid.'

'Oh?'

'The fact is . . .' She seemed both embarrassed and excited as she said, 'There's someone else who's very intrigued by what happened in Ingrid's last hours.'

She paused, controlling the narrative at her own pace. 'He's a journalist. Called Niall Connor.' A dramatic pause. 'He's my father.'

She had unleashed the revelation so dramatically that I hadn't the heart to tell her I already knew about her paternity.

'Anyway, he's been knocked sideways by the news about Ingrid's death.'

'I thought you told me you weren't in touch with him,' I said.

'No, not for a long time.' She blushed. 'But he has contacted me recently.'

'I hope that's good news.'

'Oh, it *is*. But, anyway, Niall would love to talk to you.'

'Fine.'

'So, I can give him your number?'

'Of course. It's on my website, in all the directories, under SpaceWoman.' I have no qualms about giving anyone my work number. My personal mobile I'm less generous with.

'That's great, Ellen.' She seemed disproportionately relieved. 'So . . . expect a call from Niall Connor.'

'I will.'

At that moment, our food arrived, and we settled down to the serious business of eating fish and chips. Alexandra ordered herself another Pinot Grigio.

We didn't talk much more about Ingrid Richards. Alexandra told me a few more details of her personal history. How much she'd disliked being a primary school teacher. How relieved she had been when the legacy from her grandmother had allowed her to give it up.

I discovered that the charity she worked for, on a voluntary basis, was a donkey sanctuary near Battle, just a bit north of Hastings. Apparently, she'd always liked donkeys.

Right through that lunch, though, she remained much more upbeat than she had been at our previous meeting. And I was left asking myself: Was it just her mother's death that had made her so cheerful? Or the reappearance in her life of her absent father? Or something else?

'Hello, it's Niall Connor.' There was more than a hint of Irish in his voice, which had the relaxed, deep tone of a professional charmer. 'I assume that's Ellen Curtis.'

'You assume correctly.'

'Good. "SpaceWoman" had me expecting Svetlana Savitskaya.'

I had got used to most of the witticisms surrounding the company name (for which I have to thank Ben originally), but only a journalist would have referenced the Russian cosmonaut.

'Well, I'm afraid you've got me,' I said.

'I am very fortunate to have got you.' It was a cheesy line, but his air of sending himself up took the edge off it. 'Alex told you I might call?'

'She did.' I wondered if he'd always called her 'Alex'. Or if he'd ever spoken to her before her that week?

'It is, needless to say, in relation to Ingrid Richards' death that I'm calling. You know my connection with . . .?'

'Ingrid told me.'

'Right. Well, that was all a long time ago, but I'm surprised by how much I have been shaken by the news about Ingrid. We did see a lot of each other for a while and, of course, I had great admiration for her as a journalist.'

'I've been reading the obituaries,' I said. 'I didn't know the half of her achievements.'

'No. Once Ingrid had been created, they broke the mould.'

'Yes.' There was a silence. 'So, what do you want to ask me?'

'I wonder,' he said, 'would it be possible for us to meet?'

'I don't see why not. But you're based in London, aren't you?'

'Yes, Primrose Hill. But the thing is, Ellen, my wife Grace and I also have a country place, down near Petworth.'

'Ah.'

'And you're Chichester, are you not?'

'Yes.'

'Well, listen, here's a suggestion. Grace and I are driving down to Petworth this evening. Might you be able to join us for lunch there tomorrow?'

Normally, I try to keep my weekends free of work. But was talking to Alexandra Richards' father work or not? The way I saw it, I was being offered an opportunity to find out more about a subject with which I was becoming increasingly intrigued.

Ingrid Richards' death.

I agreed to the lunch.

ELEVEN

I use the satnav a lot in the Yeti. West Sussex contains some substantial towns but outside them the population density is a lot thinner. There are few house numbers and lots of house names. I pride myself on punctuality and keying a postcode into the satnav is the best way of ensuring it.

Petworth's a pretty little town which spreads out from Petworth House and Park, now owned by the National Trust. A bit like Arundel, it's a great place if you want to buy an antique brass warming pan or a cream tea, but is not so well stocked with essentials. For their basic shopping, most residents drive their SUVs to supermarkets in less genteel parts of the county.

I was guided to the address Niall Connor had given me, buried in the South Downs, off a side road between Petworth and Fittleworth. The house had a frontage of Georgian rectangular symmetries. A gravelled parking area surrounded a circular space of carefully cultivated wild-flower garden. It looked familiar. I somehow felt I had encountered its perfection before.

One o'clock had been suggested and I arrived on the dot, just as I would have done for a business meeting. Perhaps this was a business meeting. I wouldn't be able to say until Niall Connor told me what he wanted to talk about.

I had to wait before my ring at the old-fashioned bell-pull was answered and the way Niall Connor slouched against the doorway suggested the delay had been deliberate. His keeping me waiting expressed some kind of power game or one-upmanship. He had the look of someone who liked to be in control.

Not wanting to make the mistake I had with Ingrid Richards, I'd done my Wikipedia homework on him. In many ways, their journalistic careers had followed similar trajectories, though he was some eight years younger. They had covered many of the same wars and conflicts and had no doubt been frequently thrown together in terrifying circumstances. Offering plenty of opportunities for we-might-die-tomorrow sexual encounters.

Niall Connor's journalistic career had been hugely successful. He'd won lots of awards for his intrepid reportage. His greatest coup had been in 1986, when he'd sprung the British hostage, fellow journalist Paul McClennan, from his captors in Beirut. As soon as I saw the name the details came back to me. The escape plan had involved Niall Connor in complex secret contacts, bribery of McClennan's captors, a hazardous drive across the war-torn city with the released hostage in his car boot and smuggling him on to an aeroplane. The climax had been a triumphal media-crowded arrival to Heathrow. The photograph of Niall Connor raising the arm of Paul McClennan as they stepped off the plane was one of the iconic images of the 1980s, almost on a par with the fall of the Berlin Wall.

The exploit had led to a predictable circus of press and television coverage. The inevitable book had followed, written by Niall Connor 'with the cooperation of Paul McClennan'. It sold in its millions to a public who seemed in those days to have an insatiable appetite for hostage stories. There was even a movie, in which the parts of Connor and McClennan were taken by two very good-looking Hollywood A-listers.

This daring escapade had raised Niall Connor's status from a respected English war correspondent to an internationally known guru of journalism. His byline on a report was highly sought-after the world over. That one scoop had also considerably raised his market value and the success of the hostage story had a powerful effect on the sales of the many books he subsequently produced about various international wars and crises.

Paul McClennan soon dropped off the public radar. Traumatized by his hostage experience, he had no taste for the ferocious public scrutiny it brought him. He gave up journalism and, after a series of mental breakdowns, changed his name and lived the life of a recluse.

Whereas Niall Connor luxuriated in his enhanced profile.

The big difference between him and Ingrid Richards,

however, was that, while she had been a fixture on the television screens of every family in the country, almost all of Niall Connor's work had been in print. So, though he looked vaguely familiar when I met him, he did not have that Ingrid Richards instant recognition factor.

He must once have been a strikingly attractive man, and wasn't looking bad in his late sixties. He had the manner of someone who'd never doubted his attractiveness, an arrogance which he had learned to leaven with charm. His hair had all once been black and, though he was greying round the edges and at the back where it nestled on top of his collar, there was still some blackness in the lock that flopped over his forehead. His face was weather-beaten – or life-beaten – but his lips were surprisingly full, almost feminine.

He wore an open-necked denim shirt, under a crumpled linen jacket, frayed round the lapels and cuffs. The bottoms of his jeans were frayed too, drawing attention to the fact that he wore no socks under his faded navy deck shoes. The impression was of shabbiness, but very calculated shabbiness.

The appearance of Grace Bellamy, who had just entered the hall behind her husband, was equally calculated but in a very different way. I know roughly how old she was. Ingrid, after all, had told me she'd written a book about her own menopause. *For God's sake!* But Grace had been very expensively buffered against the depredations of age. In fact, she looked as if she'd just stepped out of the pages of a magazine.

Which, of course, in a way, she had. I recognized her much more immediately than I did Niall because, almost as long as I can remember, I'd been reading features by her. Magazines, colour supplements, everywhere. And the centre of them all was her own life. I'd read about her sleep deprivation with a teething baby – clearly from a marriage before her current one – when I was going through the same problem with Juliet. I'd empathized with her difficulties over what to cook when a dinner guest espoused vegetarianism (a much rarer occurrence back then than it is now). I'd disagreed with her over how tight a leash teenage children should be kept on. I'd been given God-knows-how-many collections of her columns as Christmas presents.

No, it was no surprise she'd written a book about her own menopause.

It struck me too that that was why I'd recognized the frontage of the house. I must have seen it in a colour supplement somewhere, no doubt in a feature by Grace Bellamy on 'Second Home Secrets'.

As I was led through the hall ('How to Make your Entrance Entrancing') to the large kitchen at the back of the house ('By Hook or By Cook'), I was impressed by how long Grace Bellamy had managed to get paid for having opinions about everything.

I was also impressed by how perfectly preserved she was. No, that's the wrong word, 'preserved' makes me think of gates and creosote. 'Well-maintained' doesn't hack it, either. '*Soigné*' is probably the best – or actually, in her case, remembering language lessons at school, *soignée*. The French do descriptions of women better than we do. Grace was in a pale blue cotton top and light grey linen trousers, dressed down for the country but still ready to face a photographer.

I got the feeling the kitchen had once been two or more separate rooms. Now it had a cooking area focused on the Aga, a sitting area focused on two deep sofas, and a dining area focused on a long pine table. There was a Belfast sink, a butcher's block and a lot of tall vases full of grasses. No discordant modern elements like steel and glass, though I bet lots of that was on display in their London home. Again, the country kitchen was all ready for the moment the colour supplement camera clicked.

Slumped by the Aga was an endearingly tatty Golden Retriever ('Is yours a Town Dog or a Country Dog?'). Grace introduced him to me as Trigorin. Of course.

'Anyway, first things first,' said Niall histrionically. 'A drink! What is the weekend for if not for drinking?' He turned to me. 'So, Ellen . . . I may call you Ellen, I hope?'

'Of course.'

'What is your particular poison? I'm already on the red wine, as you see.' He raised a glass as an unnecessary visual aid. 'But we have champagne, white wine, beer, whisky, gin, vodka and probably a lot of obscure Balkan and Middle Eastern spirits. What it is to be?'

'A glass of red wine would be nice, thank you.'

'Red wine it is.' He strode across to the surface beside the Aga, on which stood glasses and a half-empty bottle of Burgundy. As he poured my drink, he turned to Grace. 'And what will it be for you, my child bride?'

'I'll get myself some white,' she replied.

'Topped up, no doubt, with sparkling water?' Niall sneered.

'Topped up, indeed, with sparkling water,' Grace said evenly. She spoke as someone who was used to his sneers and didn't rise to them.

'Why didn't the Lord God supply me with a wife who enjoyed a drink?' He aimed the question at me, but I don't think he was expecting a response. He certainly didn't get one.

Handing my glass across, he said, 'Slump on a sofa.'

He slumped beside me. 'Ingrid enjoyed a drink. I think we should raise a glass to her. God knows there were enough times I wished her dead, but now I've got what I wanted . . . In the immortal words of Joni Mitchell, "You don't know what you've got till it's no longer there".'

I couldn't tell whether he knew he was misquoting or not. 'Anyway, let's raise a glass to Ingrid.' He looked in the direction of the Aga. 'You too, Grace.'

'I haven't poured myself a drink yet.'

'Then we'll just wait till you do.'

There was a weariness in his tone. I felt they were playing out some marital game to which I didn't know the rules. Whether Grace was needled by Niall's passive-aggressive manner to her was hard to tell. Who could divine what went on behind that immaculately made-up façade? Grace Bellamy must have had a view of the recently deceased Ingrid Richards, on whom her husband had fathered a child, but I couldn't see that ever being revealed to an outsider. Such a disclosure could shatter the carefully built-up image of domestic serenity.

Grace did not hurry getting her drink. I could see that she barely dampened the bottom of her glass with white wine and was lavish with the sparkling water. 'I'm ready now,' she announced calmly.

'Right.' Niall did not get up from the sofa as he raised his glass. 'To Ingrid! We shall not look upon her like again.'

'Ingrid!' Grace and I echoed. I touched my glass to Niall's. Grace was too far away to clink.

My first sip told me that the burgundy was of very high quality. Niall Connor as a wine snob? Yes, that would figure.

He turned his lazy, condescending eyes on me. 'So, Ellen . . . you only met the red-haired temptress the once, did you?'

'Yes.'

'And she charmed the pants off you, I dare say?'

'I did take an instant liking to her, yes.'

'So did everyone. So did I, come to that. I must've done, mustn't I, considering the outcome? The liking didn't last, though.'

He was looking at me, but he also knew that Grace, busying herself at the Aga, was hearing every word.

Seeming to read my thoughts, he went on, 'So aren't I lucky that I found a nice, cosy, biddable little wife with whom to escape the clutches of that energy vampire?'

Grace did not react, and I made no comment.

'But the more important thing, Ellen, is not so much whether you liked Ingrid as whether you thought the Brunswick Square flat was a firetrap.'

I didn't answer, so he nudged, 'And what was your professional assessment?'

I gave pretty much the same answer as I had to the detective sergeant. 'There was a lot of flammable material there, but I got the impression Ingrid was well aware of the risk.'

'Maybe that would once have been true, but as she got older and frailer . . .'

'"Frail" is the last word I would have used to describe Ingrid Richards.'

'Hm.' Niall had finished his wine. He reached for the bottle and topped himself up. Then he looked at me and offered it. I shook my head.

And decided it was my turn to ask some questions. 'When did you last see Ingrid, Niall?'

'Why do you ask?'

'Because you suggested you knew that she was getting "older and frailer".'

'I didn't have to have seen her to make that assumption.

I know how old she is – was. Always eight years older than me. That's not going to change, is it? So, at seventy-five she could well have been starting to get frail. Women tend to get brittle bones and all that, don't they?'

I wasn't about to take issue with this sweeping statement about women's health. 'As I say, Ingrid looked pretty robust to me.'

'And what about the marbles?'

'All firmly in place.'

'So, the fact that at times she almost raised self-neglect to an art form . . .?'

'Seemed to have done her no harm at all.'

'Except, of course, now she's dead. So, something's done her some harm.'

'Yes,' I agreed.

Our conversation was interrupted by Grace suggesting we moved to the table. Lunch was ready.

And, of course, it too could have been photographed for a cookbook. Chicken tagine with almonds and apricots. Couscous, a salad of peas, broad beans and, yes, edamame beans. I can cook but these days I'd very rarely go to that kind of trouble. Truth is, I'm usually cooking for just me. And that's a pleasure of diminishing returns.

For the first bit of the lunch, Niall took it upon himself to entertain me with anecdotes of dangerous times in foreign parts. They were well-polished stories and he told them well. Grace reacted as if they were new to her, for which I gave her full marks. In his day, and after a few drinks, Oliver had been an expert and very funny raconteur, so I had been cast in Grace's role, never revealing that I'd heard it all before. Many times.

I politely refused refills of my glass, but Niall had soon polished off the first bottle of Burgundy and picked up another which had already been opened. With identical label, I noticed. I felt sure that, underneath us, there was a well-stocked cellar.

Grace was making her very diluted spritzer last. She was extremely – almost excessively – pleasant to me, but I couldn't lose awareness of the distance between us. I got the impression that she was one of those people who's so accomplished

no one ever gets close to them. Though maybe Niall did. Or
didn't.

Having recharged his glass from the new bottle, he homed
back in on the subject of Ingrid Richards.

'Ellen, when you said you thought she was risk-aware, did
you mean you thought she was unlikely to have started the
fire by accident?'

'That's exactly what I meant.' Then, feeling that might sound
a bit bald, I added, 'But unlikely things do happen.'

'Oh, they do, sure. You don't need to tell a war correspondent
that.'

'Incidentally,' I said, 'I think even more unlikely is the
possibility that Ingrid might have deliberately lit the fire
herself.'

'Ellen, I'm with you all the way there. She had a very
well-developed instinct for self-preservation – not to mention
self-love. And she was far too curious about the future to
want to top herself.'

'I agree.' I didn't say more. I wanted to know in which
direction he was angling the conversation. There was certainly
something he wanted from me. An opinion, a vindication . . .?
I didn't know.

'So,' Niall continued, 'if you're ruling out an accident . . .'

'I didn't rule it out. Just said I thought it was unlikely.'

'I stand corrected, Ellen. And you also rule out – or perhaps
consider unlikely – the notion of suicide . . .'

'I do.'

'As do I. So, what are we left with?'

I could now see where he was heading and cut to the chase.
'The possibility that someone else lit the fire . . .'

'Ah. Yes.'

'Which could perhaps make Ingrid Richards' death a case
of murder.'

'So it could, Ellen. And, if we were to pursue this rather
fanciful – but appealing – conjecture, I think our reading of
crime fiction would provide the question we should ask next.'

'Who done it?'

'Yes. Exactly. And are you, Ellen, at this moment in a
position to name any suspects?'

'No,' I said firmly. I had my own views, but this was not a game for more than one player in which I wished to participate.

'Probably very wise.' Niall Connor noticed that his glass needed topping up again. This time he didn't even make the gesture of offering me more.

'Have you noticed,' he said, as if he were broaching a new subject, 'how cheerful Alex has seemed since the news of Ingrid's death?'

I couldn't deny that I had.

'Now, Ellen, I make no claims to have been a good father to the girl. Complete absence from a child's life is not the route recommended in most parenting books. But I think, from the girl's point of view, Ingrid's track record is at least as bad.'

I had views on this but kept them to myself.

'In the crime novels we were talking about just then,' he observed, 'the first suspect is always the last person to see the victim alive.'

Having planted the suspicion, he left it at that. The conversation opened out. Grace contributed more to it. She talked about her weekend plans for the garden, which was as perfectly maintained as everything else in her life. (Including her marriage? I asked myself again.)

I couldn't go far up that conversational avenue with her. Not gardening. The garden at the house in Chichester is unadorned and functional. Everything was cut back in the days when the children still played *in* it, and since then I haven't had time to play *with* it. I was never much interested in gardens, anyway. I get my energy from people, not plants.

The dessert course was predictably excellent too. Fresh soft fruit with home-made sorbets, an expertly chosen cheeseboard, impeccable coffee. They may have been pushing the boat out in my honour, but I got the feeling Grace Bellamy's perfectionism meant they always lived like that.

I found it all very pleasant but not relaxing. I was glad when the appropriate time came for me to say my goodbyes.

Niall Connor saw me out to the front door. His stood in the columned porch, his eyes screwed up against the afternoon sun.

'What do you think of my daughter?' he asked suddenly.

'Alexandra? She seems pleasant enough. I don't know her well.'

'No? You had lunch with her yesterday.'

'True. That still doesn't mean I know her.'

'No.' A silence. 'Pity her parents got all the looks in the family, wasn't it?'

This remark seemed so gratuitously unpleasant that I made no comment.

'When you had lunch,' Niall went on, 'did Alex mention the memoir Ingrid was writing?'

'No. Ingrid herself had mentioned it to me.'

'Mm. Alex didn't mention helping Ingrid with her research in any way, did she?'

'No. But that would have been very unlikely to have happened, wouldn't it? Given the way Alexandra described her relationship with her mother to me.'

'I suppose it would, yes.' But this was a bone he had to keep chewing. 'I wonder if Alex took any documentation from Brunswick Square . . .?'

'If she did, she certainly didn't mention it to me. Not that there's any reason why she should have done. Most likely any documentation there was around went up in flames along with the flat.'

'Yes, you're probably right.' I couldn't tell whether he looked relieved or regretful. 'Anyway, Ellen, one thing we can guarantee . . . in a few months' time there'll be one hell of a big memorial service for Ingrid.'

'I'm sure there will.'

'The question is: who will organize the thing? The BBC'll have something to do with it, obviously . . .' He seemed to be talking to himself rather than me.

'And presumably Alexandra will be involved?'

'I suppose she'll have to be there,' he said grudgingly.

'I meant involved in the organization.'

'God, no. She'd make a right pig's breakfast of it. No, we'll probably have to sort it out.'

'We?'

'Grace and I. By which I mean Grace. She's much better at that organizational stuff than I am.'

I didn't doubt it. But there still seemed something odd about the idea of Grace Bellamy organizing a memorial service for the mother of her husband's illegitimate child.

'Look,' said Niall, 'let me give you a card. All our contacts, you know, if you do . . . if you hear anything . . .'

I didn't look at the card in detail then – I did later – but I was struck by the fact that it was for both of them – 'Niall Connor and Grace Bellamy'. I thought that was odd. They were both still working, they must have had individual business cards. But this one, presumably to be given to new private acquaintances like me, seemed like it was asserting the strength of their marriage.

Given what Ingrid Richards had said about Niall's habitual womanizing, I wondered how faithful he had been to Grace.

Tucking the card in my pocket, I said, 'Sorry, I must go, thanks so much for the lunch. And do thank Grace again.'

'Yes, of course,' he said distractedly. And then, 'God, I'm going to miss Ingrid.'

I looked up at him and saw, to my surprise, that there were tears in Niall Connor's eyes.

TWELVE

My encounter with Niall and Grace had left me unsettled, wondering why they had actually wanted to see me. I say 'they', but I really mean 'he'. I don't think Grace did particularly want to see me, but her professionally civilized manner would never allow her to show it.

It was Niall's questions, though, that had left me unsettled, and I tried to analyse them as I drove back to Chichester. I could understand why he wanted to talk to me about the fire risk in the Brunswick Square flat, because that was the reason for my visit to Ingrid. In a business capacity. But he could have asked me about that on the phone. It hadn't required the full charm offensive of Grace's exquisite lunch.

He had also definitely been sounding me out about Alexandra's role in the proceedings. Even pushing me towards the idea that she might have had a role in her mother's death. Which would have worried me less if I hadn't already got suspicions of my own moving in that direction.

A rather unpleasant chain of logic was forming in my mind. If one were being profoundly cynical, which I'm not by nature but have occasionally had to be, one might see a pattern. Alexandra had only called me in to check on her mother's risk status, so that I could testify to the danger, in the event of something happening to Ingrid. In retrospect, it was striking how quickly both the police and Niall Connor had contacted me for my views. And the only person who could have put them on to me was Alexandra.

Which meant of course that she might have been planning—

My mobile rang. I looked at the in-car display. Ben.

I answered immediately.

'Hello, Ma,' he said in that languid, sending-up voice I so love.

'Look, I'm in the car. I'll find somewhere to park.'

'All that hands-free technology is wasted on you, isn't it,

Ma? The best minds in Silicon Valley worked for years to produce the ultimate high-tec safe in-car phone system, only for Ellen Curtis to pronounce that it's not good enough for her.'

'Ha ha,' I said drily, as I edged the Yeti into a layby. 'All right, I'm a dinosaur. But I can't concentrate on driving and talking on the phone at the same time. You know that.'

'If you say so, Ma.'

'Anyway . . . putting my technophobia on one side . . . how are you?'

'I'm fine.' His voice sounded worryingly light and brittle. 'And you?'

'Also fine. Just driving home after a very good lunch in Petworth.'

'Who with?' he asked sharply.

'A couple who . . . It's too complicated to explain now. And irrelevant.'

'Oh, a couple.' He larded the words with mock-disappointment. 'I thought it might be Mr Right.'

Ben has this running joke about me meeting someone else. I never know how serious he is about it. He was totally devastated by Oliver's death. On the edge of his teens when it happened, a very vulnerable age. I wonder how he would react if I did start seeing someone else . . .?

Not that he need have any worries on that score. Since being widowed, I have had my fair share of men coming on to me and, though it has led to some socially awkward problems of extrication, I've never been tempted. I think – and it's not a thought that I always find comforting – that I'm a one-man woman. And that man, sadly, is no longer available.

I treated Ben's reference to Mr Right with another dry 'Ha ha' and asked how the course was going.

'Good. I'm working on an animation project for the end of term.'

'What's it about?'

'It's funny. At least, it's meant to be funny. Hope it is. Only three minutes.'

I knew from Oliver's dabbling in animation just how long it could take to produce three minutes. 'Good luck with it.'

'I'm basing it on "Riq and Raq" . . . you know, the strip that Dad did.'

'Of course I know, Ben.'

As well as his political cartoons, Oliver had developed 'Riq and Raq' as a kind of social commentary on a young couple with a small child negotiating the difficulties of life in London. I was delighted to hear that Ben was using his father's work as an inspiration. It was rarely that he talked about Oliver. In that he was unlike his sister. Jools absolutely never talked about him.

'Yes, you would know,' said Ben. 'Anyway, I'm kind of updating that, seeing how Riq and Raq . . . or any young couple, really . . . would cope in today's world . . . with electric cars and social media and fake news.'

'Great idea.'

'Yes.' He didn't sound convinced.

'You know, of course, that "Riq and Raq" was based on us. Your father and I were Riq and Raq. And Juliet was the baby. You hadn't arrived back then.'

'No.' The brightness with which he had started the conversation seemed to have dissipated.

I couldn't stop myself from saying, 'You know, if you want to come down here for a weekend or something, you're always welcome.'

'I know that,' he said flatly.

There was a silence. I tried to jolly him along. 'And is your "Riq and Raq" also based on a real couple?'

'How do you mean?'

'Well, I thought maybe you and Tracey . . .?'

It was a clumsy way to introduce her into the conversation and probably deserved the sharp 'No' it got by way of response.

'All all right there?'

'Oh yes,' he replied airily. Too airily. 'Yes, yes, yes, yes, yes.'

I should probably have stopped digging but I couldn't. 'I do look forward to meeting Tracey some time,' I said.

'Oh. Well.' Ben sounded confused. 'There might not be much point in you doing that.'

'What do you mean? Are you not seeing her any more?'

'Who knows?' he replied unhelpfully.

'Are you saying it's over?'

'Oh no,' he replied, exactly as he had just said, 'Oh yes'. 'No, no, no, no, no.'

'Then what are you saying, Ben?'

'I'm just saying that there are plenty more fish in the sea. Plenty more pebbles on the beach. Plenty more fish on the beach. Gasping for breath,' he concluded mournfully.

'In other words, you and Tracey are no longer seeing each other?'

'Oh, by no means. What I'm saying is that we are still in theory seeing each other.'

'In theory?'

'Neither of us is seeing anyone else, but . . .'

With agonizing difficulty, I stopped myself from prompting him.

After a long silence, Ben finished his sentence. '. . . we both feel we need a little space at the moment.'

My heart sank. When speaking of relationships, 'space' is never a good word to hear.

The conversation with my son ended unsatisfactorily. He got jokey and evasive. As he had with that riff about fish and pebbles. Not to put too fine a point on it, he got manic. Which is always worrying. As it had with his father, the manic phase is always followed by something worse.

I tried to persuade Ben to come down to Chichester, just for a few days, a break. But he said he was far too busy with the deadline he'd got on his 'Riq and Raq' project. Then, with an almost brusque 'Lots of love, Ma', he rang off.

My instinct was to ring him straight back, but I curbed it. Ben was a grown-up now. Even though I knew his terrible vulnerability, I must never try to reattach the apron strings. If he felt the need to come and chill out with me for a few days in Chichester, fine. But I couldn't force the decision on him.

I felt predictably restless when I got home. I've got a substantial collection of recorded medical soaps which I watch in my rare moments of mindless downtime, but I couldn't concentrate on anything like that. I was preoccupied, not only by suspicions of Alexandra Richards, but now by worries about Ben too.

For a long time after Oliver's death, I hid away all his artwork, but gradually I'd been hanging up more of his framed cartoons. There was a particular favourite 'Riq and Raq' strip in the hall. As I looked at it, along with my anxiety about Ben, I also felt pleasure that he was using his father's work as a springboard for his own creativity. But the anxiety was stronger.

I went through to the kitchen and poured a large glass of Merlot. I'd restrained myself with Niall Connor's excellent wine at lunchtime, but now I thought I deserved a drink.

Just as I raised the glass to my lips, my mobile rang. It was Alexandra. 'Did you go and see my father?' she asked.

'The fact that you ask that question,' I said, 'means you know I did.'

'Yes,' she admitted. 'Did he say anything about me?'

She sounded so needy, it got me thinking about her relationship with Niall. He had a long history of neglecting his daughter. 'I've never seen much of my father,' as she'd said bleakly at our first meeting. Was it possible that Ingrid Richards' death might bring them closer together? If it did, the impression I'd got of Niall Connor's selfishness did not allow me to think the rapprochement would last for long.

'Yes, your name came up, obviously.'

'What did he say about me?'

I wasn't about to pass on his remark about her parents having got the family's allocation of good looks. Nor his scepticism about her ability to help organize the memorial service. I said, 'He asked if you knew about the memoir Ingrid was writing.'

'And you said I did?'

'Yes. There's no secret about it, is there?'

'No, I suppose not.' She didn't sound sure.

'He was also asking me whether you might have any of Ingrid's research documents.'

'What do you mean?'

'Just that. I don't know why he thought I might know anything about it.'

'So, let me get this right, Ellen. Niall thought I might have taken some of Ingrid's research papers? From her flat?'

'I assume that's what he meant, yes.'

'I wonder what made him think that.' But she sounded quite pleased.

'Are you saying you do have some stuff?'

'Yes, Ellen. I do.'

'Ah. Well, I got the impression that Niall might be extremely interested in it.'

'Hm . . . I wonder whether I should tell him what I've got.' She sounded playful now, as if the documentation she had taken might give her some power over her neglectful father.

'That's up to you,' I said. I didn't want to get involved, though at the same time I was achingly curious as to what the papers might reveal.

'Maybe you could advise me . . .?'

'What?'

'If you had a look at the stuff I've got, then you could tell me whether to show it to Niall or not.'

Why me, I thought. But the urge to see the stuff was strong.

'If you could come over to my place . . .' Alexandra suggested.

'When?'

'Well, this evening. I'm out now, but I'll be back home by six thirty or so.'

Back home in Hastings, for God's sake. I'd already done Chichester to Petworth and back. On the other hand, I was being offered more information about what I was increasingly thinking of as the mystery of Ingrid Richards' death. And it was a mystery that needed solving. I wouldn't rest until I knew what had actually happened.

And if I spent the evening alone at home with a bottle of Merlot, all I'd do would be to worry about Ben.

I said I'd go to Hastings.

The satnav must have expected more traffic than there was because I arrived at the address Alexandra had given me soon after six. I managed to park directly outside. It was a small house in the Old Town, probably once owned by a fisherman but now considerably refurbished. And way out of a fisherman's price range. Hastings had become something of a property hotspot. Still a bit louche, like Littlehampton, but increasingly popular with people in the creative industries.

The front window had modern leaded panes, double-glazed ones perhaps echoing the outlines of the originals. As I unclicked my seatbelt, I looked through into the sitting room.

At an open desk in the bay window, a man I'd never seen before was sitting, riffling through a pile of folders.

THIRTEEN

He was unremarkable-looking, fortyish, short, with a couple of tendrils of mousy hair trained across his bald cranium. His owl-like round glasses might have looked stylish on someone more prepossessing. He wore a T-shirt with a camouflage design in black, grey, and white.

My mind was racing. Thinking, inevitably, of the documentation Niall Connor had mentioned. It appeared that he was not the only person interested in what Alexandra had taken from her mother's flat. Or could the man going through Alexandra's papers be acting on Niall's instructions?

I was undecided for a moment what to do. Almost as soon as we'd met, Alexandra had told me that she lived alone. She'd said she'd probably be out till six thirty. So, it wasn't unreasonable to conclude that the man in her front room was an intruder.

It would, however, be ridiculous to call the police straight away. I got out my mobile to ring Alexandra. If she didn't know who the man was, then appropriate action could be taken.

But before I found her number, through the window I saw her enter the front room. Her reaction showed that she did know the man who was checking through her papers but also that she was annoyed with him. Obviously, I couldn't hear what was being said but the mime I was watching appeared to be of a row. Whether the cause of the row was his interest in her files, I couldn't judge.

Then the man stood up. He was almost a head shorter than Alexandra. He put his arms round her and kissed her on the lips.

'Ellen, this is Walt.'

He was once again sitting in front of Alexandra's desk, with her papers scattered over its surface. I was struck by how in control he seemed in her house. Knees literally under the table. There was about Walt an air of entitlement, even pomposity, at odds with his rather nerdish appearance.

'Pleased to meet you,' I said.

Walt inclined his head condescendingly towards me.

Alexandra seemed unrelaxed, anxious perhaps about how I would react to her friend. 'I didn't know Walt was going to be here when I fixed for you to come over.'

'Well, it's not a problem, is it?' he said. 'I have a key. I can come and go as I please, can't I?'

'Yes, of course you can,' she hastened to assure him.

'That's what happens when you're' – he did that annoying thing of miming inverted commas for the words – 'an item.'

'Yes, of course,' said Alexandra.

'Well, congratulations,' I said, 'on being' – I felt an unaccountable urge to send Walt up by doing the same mime myself, but I resisted it – 'an item.'

'Yes, we're incredibly lucky,' said Alexandra. 'It just happened. We met when Walt came to fix my laptop.'

That fitted. A casting director looking for someone to play a computer repair man would probably have rejected Walt as too obvious.

'Less than two months ago,' he said serenely. 'And we just clicked. Didn't we, lovie?'

'Yes, we did, lovie,' said Alexandra.

This grated on me. What they called each in private was up to them, but I didn't warm to this public winsomeness. I had very quickly got the feeling that Walt defined the parameters of their relationship. He seemed controlling. Maybe Alexandra was so unused to having someone in her life that she just went along with whatever he wanted.

Time to move things on. 'Look, I don't want to keep you, Alexandra, since you've got company. Maybe you could show me the papers you took from Ingrid's flat . . .?'

'Yes, I—'

'Just a minute,' said Walt, addressing Alexandra rather than me. 'What right has she got to look at your stuff?'

'She's got as much right as you have!' Alexandra snapped back, confirming that the disagreement I'd witnessed through the window was about his going through her papers. But as soon as the words were spoken, she backtracked. 'I'm sorry, Walt, that came out wrong.'

'Yes, it did rather,' he chided her, 'but don't worry. The reason it's all right for me to look through your stuff, lovie, is because we're an item.' He seemed to be fixated on the word. 'It's only natural at the beginning of a new and exciting relationship to want to know as much as you can about the other person. There shouldn't be any secrets between us. That's why we need to know the passcodes for each other's mobile phones. What's yours is mine, lovie.'

'Yes, of course, lovie,' said a meek Alexandra.

'But,' Walt went on, looking contemptuously at me, 'that doesn't apply to *her*.'

I'd had enough of this. Looking him straight in the eye, I said, 'I am here because Alexandra asked me to come and look at some papers from her late mother's flat. I am a professional declutterer. I know Alexandra because she contacted me about Ingrid Richards' hoarding habit and the potential fire risk in her flat.' I turned to look straight at Alexandra. 'So, either you show me the stuff you wanted me to look at or I will leave.'

'No, of course you must see it . . . having come so far.' She reached over Walt's shoulders to the piles of paper on the desk, and produced a file, once red now faded pink. Then she announced, 'I feel in need of a drink.'

'Budweiser,' said Walt.

'Can I get you something, Ellen?'

'No, thanks.' I'd wait for a large Merlot when I got back to Chichester. I felt a pang. Because, of course, when I got back to Chichester, there'd be nothing to stop me agonizing about Ben.

Alexandra had drifted through to the kitchen. Walt sat back in the desk chair, appraising me. 'I suppose it would be easier for you to read that if you sat here,' he said.

'It might.'

He nodded, making no effort to move.

'But I could do it perfectly adequately on the sofa,' I said, gliding in that direction.

'No, no, it's all right.' He stood up, gesturing over-elaborately towards the vacated chair. 'You did hear about Ally's Mum, didn't you?'

'Yes, of course I did.'

'I didn't meet her. In fact, Ally didn't mention her until after the news of her death was all over everything.'

'Really?' That sounded odd to me.

'She said she wanted our relationship to be uncluttered.'

There, of course, was a word that resonated with me. And I thought, not for the first time, how much of the emotional clutter which surrounded people was caused by other family members.

'I could see her point,' Walt went on, 'but I'd have to have found out about her mother sooner or later.'

'Did Alexandra say why she didn't mention Ingrid to you?'

'Ally didn't think we'd hit it off.'

I didn't say so, but I reckoned 'Ally's' assessment was spot on. The image of Walt swapping badinage with Ingrid Richards was too incongruous to contemplate. I wondered if another reason for keeping them apart was that Alexandra was slightly ashamed of him. Walt was way out of the league of her mother's high-profile lovers. And Ingrid, I felt pretty sure, was not a woman to suffer fools gladly.

Another possibility, of course, was that Alexandra was afraid of Walt being attracted to her mother. Even in her seventies, Ingrid Richards still exuded sexual charisma. Did her daughter fear being upstaged yet again?

'From all accounts,' Walt went on, 'by not having met her, I'm not missing much.'

I thought he was missing quite a lot. Ingrid Richards was one of the most impressive women I'd ever encountered. But again, I passed no comment.

'Apparently, she made Ally's life hell.'

That was less arguable. Ingrid's track record on the maternal front had not been impressive.

'Total lack of interest in her. Everything Ally's achieved she's had to achieve for herself.'

It would have been cruel to ask what Alexandra actually had achieved. Working for free for a donkey sanctuary?

He went on, 'She was very damaged by having a mother like that. It was deeply harmful to her mental health. When we first met, Ally was totally dependent on anti-depressants and sleeping pills. Her bathroom cabinet was full of Zopiclone. I've seen it as part of my role in the relationship to wean her off those. And to undo some of the damage inflicted by her mother.'

God, the pomposity of the little tick. Seeing things as part of his 'role in the relationship'. I squirmed inwardly.

'I think Ally's lack of self-esteem is all down to her mother. That's why she never had any successful relationships with men – the thought of Ingrid Richards peering over her shoulder all the time. No wonder Ally was still a virgin in her thirties.'

This was more information than I required – and more than he should have been sharing. But I was surprised about her age. For me, her dowdiness had put her firmly into her forties, if not older. 'How old is she actually?' I asked.

'Thirty-six,' Walt went on. 'And who knows how much longer she might have continued with her miserable existence of anti-depressants and sleeping pills. It's just incredibly fortunate for her that she met me, someone who could sort out her problems with her mother, once and for all – a caring man with an understanding of women. I do have experience of women, you know.'

Yuck. What must he be like in bed? The unwanted image came to me of him tutoring Alexandra in the best ways of bringing him sexual gratification.

'I think,' he went on, 'it was destiny that brought us together. I was put on this earth to *heal*, Ally. It's still a work-in-progress, but we'll get there.'

My inward squirm was now almost physically painful.

'I was much more fortunate with my parents,' Walt volunteered. 'They supported me in all of my ambitions. I wouldn't have set up Walter Rainbird Computing Solutions without their backing. My parents helped me achieve everything that I have achieved.'

An unworthy cynical voice inside me asked how much of an achievement becoming a computer repairman was. I'm normally more generous than that. Walt brought out the worst in me. And I didn't mind at all. I had discovered he was someone I was fully prepared to loathe.

'Sadly,' he went on, 'both my parents have passed.'

Another one using the expression I hate. I mumbled some appropriate condolence.

He continued pontificating, 'But, even though her mother was such a cow to her, this is still a difficult time for Ally.'

'Yes,' I agreed. Though I didn't see much evidence of it. Alexandra's predominant reaction to Ingrid's death seemed to have been relief.

'Fortunate that she's got me to keep an eye on her,' said Walt, as he too drifted through to the kitchen. Leaving me with the thought that it was a long time since anyone had managed to get up my nose so quickly. Normally, I'm more charitable with people, waiting, giving them a chance to display their approachable side. With Walt, though, I was prepared to make an exception.

I looked at the faded file. One corner was folded down. When I bent it back, a title was revealed in once blue, now brown felt pen. 'Alexandra.'

The contents were pitifully meagre. A birth certificate with a blank where the father's name could be. A sheet of four machine-taken passport photographs of a spotty early teenage Alexandra, from which one had been scissored off. A tasteless birthday card of cake and balloons bearing the legend 'To the Best Mum in the World', inscribed inside with childish letters reading, 'LOVE ALEXANDRA'. A couple of school reports.

And that was it. Nothing there to cause Niall Connor any anxiety.

I looked up from the desk to see Alexandra approaching from the kitchen, gulping from a large glass of white wine.

'You see?' she said, her eyes sparkling needily. 'So, Ingrid did really care about me, didn't she?'

I put on music in the car on the way back to Chichester. Billie Holiday. One of Oliver's favourites. I used to joke with him, however bad you're feeling, listen to some Billie Holiday and you'll realize that there's someone worse off than you.

Slit-your-wrists music, he called it. Which, as things turned out, was ironic, really.

The music didn't distract me as much as I'd hoped, though. Take more than Billie Holiday to stop me thinking. So, trying to keep my thoughts away from Ben, I focused on Alexandra and Walt.

I was glad for her sake that she had at least got someone. I could not pretend the someone she'd got was to my liking. Horses for courses, though. I knew lots of remarkably successful relationships between people, neither of whom scored high on the accepted attractiveness scale. But in this case, Walt's manner rang warning bells. I hoped that Alexandra, who perhaps hadn't a lot of experience of relationships, knew what she was getting herself into. Being the object of affection for someone like Walt could come at a cost. He was definitely controlling.

I wondered, though, whether it was Walt's presence in her life that seemed to have made Alexandra more cheerful. Or was that down to renewed contact from her absent father? Or possibly both?

And had her improved mood maybe given Alexandra the confidence to confront what she had come to regard as a blight on her life, the existence of her mother? Even to the extent of suggesting an extreme way of solving that problem once and for all . . .?

But no. I was going too fast. I was overreacting to the suspicions of Alexandra that Niall Connor had sown in my mind.

As soon as I got back home, I poured the large glass of Merlot I'd been promising myself all the way from Hastings. Maybe I could distract myself with one of my medical soaps now?

My mobile rang. I recognized the number as Mary Griffin's. 'It's Dodge,' she said. 'I think he's dead.'

FOURTEEN

I could see that Dodge wasn't dead but he was in a bad way. It was by then after ten on the Saturday evening, which meant the streets of Ferring were totally deserted. Buttoned-up and sniffy, the village wasn't one of the late-night hotspots of the Costa Geriatrica.

Dodge lay on the pavement between Mary Griffin's front door and his Morris Tipper. There was blood everywhere.

Mary had been hysterical when she rang me. She was unable to give a coherent account of what happened. I couldn't even gather whether she'd witnessed the attack. Whether she'd phoned the police or called for an ambulance. Basically, she was terrified. I'd told her to wait indoors till I joined her there.

I'd parked the Yeti next to the van and left the headlights on, so that I could see the scene of the crime. And, as soon as I looked at Dodge, I knew that a crime had been committed.

He had suffered a severe beating. I think most of the blood spattered over his sweatshirt had dripped down from his head wounds. Whether there were open cuts on other parts of his body, I couldn't see.

But the face had taken a vicious battering. It looked like that of a boxer just before the fight was stopped. His eyebrows were split and swollen. So were his lips. His nose was a shapeless mass, like butcher's meat. The backs of his hands were cut and bloody, presumably from attempts to protect himself.

The beam of my headlights glinted on the fresh blood but also on the eyes whose lashes flickered. Which told me he was alive.

'Dodge,' I whispered, 'are you all right?'

Even as I said the words, I realized what a stupid question it was. I had only to look at him to see that he was far from all right.

'Been better.' The reply cheered me. Not only did it prove he was conscious, it also had an edge of humour to it. I also realized that, because of his limited mobility, Dodge was actually looking me in the eye. For the first time in our relationship. So that's what it took.

'Has Mary called an ambulance?' I asked.

'No, I told her not to.'

'But, Dodge, you're in no state—'

'I don't want to get caught up in the system,' he said, in a voice that brooked no argument.

I didn't like leaving Mary Griffin on her own, but Dodge's need was greater. He winced with pain as I got him upright but did not allow himself to cry out. Then I manhandled him into the back of the Yeti, having first covered the seats with a waterproof sheet. (My car's well used to carrying messy detritus, so I'm equipped for most eventualities. Fortunately, the threat to its upholstery is not often blood.)

Telling Dodge I wouldn't be long, I went to check on Mary. She was still in a terrible state but I managed to get from her that she hadn't actually witnessed the attack. Dodge had arrived early evening with a desk he'd made for Amy, again decorated with *Frozen* stickers. Mary had offered him something to eat or a drink, but he'd refused and said he had to get back.

It was only when she'd gone upstairs to check Amy was asleep that she'd seen the Morris Tipper was still parked outside and gone to investigate. Her first instinct had been to call for an ambulance, but Dodge had managed to persuade her against the idea, just as he had me. So, she knew he wasn't dead. What she'd said to me on the phone was a by-product of hysteria.

The reason for that hysteria was her conviction that her husband had attacked Dodge. I tried to persuade her that was impossible because Craig was locked up in prison, but her mind wasn't receptive to logic.

I asked if she'd got anyone, family, or friend, who could come to sit with her, but there wasn't anyone. As is so often the case with coercive partners, Craig Griffin's controlling jealousy had made her cut off all contacts of that kind. I found myself wondering whether Walt would do the same for Alexandra. But then I hadn't got the impression she had much of a social circle, anyway.

All I could do was to tell Mary Griffin to make sure the house was securely locked up. I said I'd ring in the morning.

By the time I got back to the Yeti, Dodge had fallen asleep. Probably best thing for him. He'd mumbled as I got him into the car that he wanted me to drive back to his place, but there was no way I was going to do that. Not until I'd checked the extent of his injuries, anyway. If they were really bad, I was determined to overrule his resistance to calling an ambulance. I had no desire for him to die on me.

His body had stiffened up on the drive to Chichester and he was clearly in a lot of pain as I manoeuvred him into the house. But the fact that he could stand and move, albeit with difficulty, suggested no bones were broken.

As he leant against me in the hall, he said, 'I asked you to take me back to my place.'

'I know you did. But there's no way I'm going to do that until I've cleaned you up a bit.'

Fear sparked in his eyes as he said, 'While I was asleep in the car, you didn't call an ambulance, did you?'

I reassured him that I hadn't. 'Dodge, do you think you can make it up the stairs to the bathroom?'

'I can try.'

It was hard, and I was glad of the fitness that constantly moving cardboard boxes about had given me. The blood had stopped flowing so my carpets didn't suffer much. Not that I would have minded if they had. I like the house to be clean but I'm not obsessive about it. That's a gene I don't have, though Jools does. Everywhere she lives is almost antiseptically tidy. Another point of difference between mother and daughter.

I got Dodge to the bathroom and ran hot water into the basin. I produced towels from the airing cupboard and laid one on the floor. 'It'll get filthy,' he protested.

'That's what towels are for. Come on, let's get everything off and see the damage.'

Removing his clothes, I was as gentle as I could be. Getting his trainers off was easy. Next the socks, which were thick with blood. Jeans no problem, belt, and zip. Underneath he wore old-fashioned white Y-fronts, also spattered with blood.

But getting his sweatshirt over his battered head was going to be trickier. I reached for a pair of hairdressing scissors which I sometimes use to tidy up my fringe. 'Going to be easier to cut you out of this.'

'Don't you dare,' said Dodge, characteristically putting the health of the planet above his own comfort. 'There's still years of wear in that sweatshirt.'

Obediently, I edged it up over his head. Then the T-shirt he wore underneath. Both had been washed so many times that it was impossible to guess at their original colour. Both were rusted with blood.

The scraping of fabric against Dodge's head wounds started some of them bleeding again. I looked at him in shock.

There were few open wounds on the rest of his body, but it was a patchwork of swellings. Most were still red, but some had started to take on the darker discolouration of bruising. Thank God, a cursory examination seemed to confirm that no bones had been broken, though there might be fractures in his hands, which had been stamped on.

Dodge stood still on the towel while, as delicately as I knew how, I used a face cloth to sponge him down, starting at the lacerated head. The cloth filled quickly with blood and I had to keep rinsing it.

Dodge tensed when the wounds stung. He must have been in terrible pain, but still he did not cry out.

I slipped off the bloodied Y-fronts to reveal swollen testicles which had undergone a fierce kicking. I could not imagine how great that pain was.

It struck me, with perverse timing, that this was the first time since Oliver's death that I'd been in a room with a naked adult man. Never had a situation felt less sexual.

'Who did this to you, Dodge?'

'I don't know.'

'Who could possibly do this to another human being?'

'I don't know.'

'Whoever did it is still out there. And, God knows, quite

capable of doing it to someone else. He must be stopped. We must call the police.'

'No. I don't want to get caught up in the system,' Dodge repeated stubbornly.

I finally persuaded him that, though he was desperate to be back in his own place, he was in no condition to travel any further that night. The bed was made up in Ben's room (reflecting my slightly pathetic hope that he'd suddenly turn up one day). Dodge could stay there overnight. I promised I wouldn't contact either medical or police services until we'd had a talk in the morning.

Having cleaned him up, I was able to see more clearly the injuries to his head. They weren't as bad as I'd feared – facial wounds do always produce a disproportionate amount of blood. There were a couple of gashes on his eyebrows which I thought might need stitches but I didn't tell him that. He was at first unwilling to have plasters put on any of the cuts. Dodge believed in naturopathic medicine and didn't like using anything produced by the pharmaceutical industry. I only persuaded him to have the plasters on by saying it was to protect Ben's sheets and pillows.

Dodge had the same reaction when I offered him a sleeping pill. I'd had some Zopiclone prescribed by my GP during those terrible months after Oliver's death. They were way beyond their expiry date but still might have helped him to sleep through the pain. But he rejected them, anyway.

He also refused the offer of an alcoholic drink. The Merlot was still open and in a kitchen cupboard there was a bottle of whisky, another precaution in case my son suddenly appeared. Ben liked his whisky. Perhaps too much. I sometimes worried about his consumption of alcohol. Oliver had had his battles with the booze and Ben was like his father in so many other ways . . .

I'd found Dodge an ancient pair of Ben's pyjamas. Since he was a good eight inches taller than my son, they looked slightly ridiculous on him. But they did cover the worst of the bruises.

We were still in the bathroom. Dodge said he could manage

to get to Ben's room on his own. He said he'd just have a pee and then go to bed. I hoped peeing wasn't going to be too agonizing for him.

As I gathered up the bloodied clothes, towels, and face cloth, he said, 'Sorry to have made such a mess, Ellen.'

It was long after midnight. I was tired but not yet ready for bed. I put everything of Dodge's in the machine on a hot wash and sat down in the kitchen to drink the glass of Merlot I'd abandoned when Alexandra Richards rang, in what felt like another lifetime. Back then I'd put a saucer on it to keep off the flies and it still tasted fine.

I took a long, grateful swallow and finally confronted the tangle of thoughts which had been building up in my mind.

The beating-up of Dodge. The identity of his assailant. There was an unpleasant chain of logic developing there, which I didn't want to confront.

And, of course, Dodge's unwillingness to get 'caught up in the system'. That I'm sure was another reaction to the breakdown he'd had which had ended his career in the City. From the minimal information he had volunteered about that time, and from the fact that he now worked as a counsellor for a Portsmouth drug rehabilitation charity called ReProgramme, I reckoned drugs must have been involved. Which would explain his unwillingness to have anything to do with the police. But what his objection to the NHS was, I had no idea. Maybe he'd been scarred by some treatment he'd received and that had turned him against traditional medicine. I had no means of knowing.

I still thought, given the savagery of the attack, the police should be informed. But that argument with Dodge could wait till the morning.

Next on my disturbing thought list was the suspicion that Alexandra Richards might have had a hand in her mother's death. A thought which had been uncomfortably around since I first heard the news of the fire in Brunswick Square. But which had been given more definite shape by what Niall Connor had said.

With the suspicion came the unpleasant feeling that I might

have been set up by Alexandra. That she had only contacted me so I could confirm to the police that Ingrid Richards lived in a firetrap. Which would have cast me in the unenviable role of a pawn in Alexandra's game of murder.

But, more powerful than all of these was my anxiety about Ben's mental state. First and foremost, always, I am a mum. And, given the family history with Oliver . . .

I knew I wouldn't sleep unaided that night.

I took one of the expired Zopiclones. It worked.

It was a long time since I'd taken a sleeping pill and I woke up muzzy and disoriented. My first thought on hearing someone moving about downstairs was that I'd been burgled. Then the events of the previous evening came back to me. I slipped on my dressing gown and went down.

Dodge was standing in the kitchen, supporting himself against the table. He looked ghastly, the paleness of his face emphasizing the bruises and cuts, from which he had removed the plasters. The redness of his injuries had turned overnight to a kaleidoscope of greens, yellows and purples. He was dressed in his own clothes, which meant he'd been up for long enough to take the washing out of the machine and tumble-dry it.

When I entered the room, he looked away. That moment of eye contact we'd had when he was lying on the ground was not about to be repeated.

'How're you feeling?' I asked.

'Fine,' he lied.

'Did you get any sleep?'

'A bit.' Probably another lie. Then, urgently, 'Can you take me back to my place?'

'Now?'

'As soon as you can.'

'But I don't want to leave you there in the state you're in.'

'Please!'

I knew better than to argue with Dodge. It was something we had never done. I was aware that he was a complex of neuroses, some of which I began to understand. But I also knew of his suspicion – possibly even fear – of people. He was permanently uneasy in company, even my company. Though he was the least aggressive person I had ever met, I didn't want to cross him. I valued his friendship far too much to put it at risk.

'All right,' I said. 'Just let me put some clothes on. If you want anything to eat or drink . . .'

'No, thanks.'

I looked at his split and swollen lips. 'Does it hurt too much to swallow?'

'I'm fine,' said Dodge, lying again.

I could tell from his wincing how much the journey hurt. Bruising is always more painful on the second day. I tried to guide the Yeti as smoothly as possible but there were a lot of winter potholes that hadn't been mended on the back roads to Walberton. Each one sent an agonizing shudder through him, but still Dodge didn't cry out.

I tried to get him to talk. 'You're sure about not seeing a doctor? I could take you to A & E at St Richard's.'

'No, thank you,' he said. 'I'll sort myself out. I've got everything I need back at my place.'

'Herbal stuff?'

'Yes. Comfrey's good. Also called "knit-bone". Did you know that?'

I confessed that I didn't.

'It works. I don't think I've got any broken bones, but it's also good as an anti-inflammatory. Inhibits infection too.'

'Do you use arnica?' I asked.

'A bit, but I've found other things more effective.'

'Like?'

'Aloe vera, parsley . . . cabbage.'

'Cabbage?' I echoed in amazement.

'Yes. The humble cabbage. Make compresses with it. Good for bruises.'

The Yeti turned in the narrow track that led to his home. 'Dodge,' I said, 'I've got to ask you. Do you have any idea who attacked you?'

'No,' he mumbled, avoiding eye contact more than ever.

I couldn't stop myself from saying, 'It isn't anything to do with drugs, is it?'

'What do you mean?'

'Look, I know you're involved in that ReProgramme thing in Portsmouth . . .'

'Yes.' It wasn't something he liked to talk about.

'Well, I just wondered if, through that, you might have got on the wrong side of some drug dealers or . . .'

'No,' he said. 'The attack was nothing to do with that.'

I brought the Yeti to a halt in the space between the house and the two corrugated-iron-roofed outbuildings. 'Then what did it have to do with?'

'I don't know.'

I couldn't tell whether that was the truth or not. 'But surely you must want to know who did that to you . . .?'

'No,' he said.

'You must be curious. Just to know his identity. I'm not talking about seeking revenge or—'

'I don't believe in revenge,' he said.

I was beginning to get quite angry with him. 'Dodge, I've heard about turning the other cheek, but this is ridiculous. You can't just accept a savage beating like that without wanting to know the reason for it.'

'Shit happens.' He began to shrug, then realized that the movement would be too painful. 'I must get my van back,' he said.

'Yes, I'm sure I can sort out some way of doing that. If you give me the key . . .'

'At least,' he went on, as he handed the key over, 'whoever it was didn't touch the van. He probably didn't realize it belonged to me.'

I keep getting close to thinking I understand Dodge, and then he says something which instantly dismantles everything I've ever thought about him. Like what he just said then. It sounded as if he was more concerned about the survival of his 1951 Morris Commercial CV9/40 Tipper than he was about his own.

Which, knowing Dodge – as I inadequately do – was entirely possible.

I stopped in a layby on the A27 to call Mary Griffin. Things with her were as I had feared. She sounded more paranoid than ever.

'It was Craig,' she said.

'What was Craig?'

'Dodge. Craig did that.'

'Mary, you know that's impossible. Craig is in prison and he's going to stay in prison for some time yet. You're quite safe from him.'

'No, I'm not.'

'What do you mean?'

'The man who attacked Dodge, he'd just come out of the same nick. Craig set him up to watch the house. He'd heard from someone that Dodge had been seen here. Only delivering furniture for Amy, but Craig was never going to believe that, was he? So, he set up this ex-con to give a beating to any man who came out of the house . . . and poor Dodge . . .' She was overcome by hysterical tears.

'Mary,' I said, 'maybe it's time we called the police.'

I was worried about betraying Dodge, but in fact Mary was even more against the idea than he had been. 'No. Craig would find out! We mustn't call the police!'

'Are you sure Craig was behind the attack? Do you have any proof?'

'He texted me.'

'Craig? From the prison?'

'Yes. God knows how he managed it.'

'What did the text say?'

Controlling her emotion, she read: 'That's what'll happen to any other man you start seeing behind my back. You're still my wife, Mary, and it's about time you started behaving like my wife.'

'Oh, Ellen,' cried Mary Griffin, 'I'm so terrified!'

I saw it as soon as I opened the front door. A familiar back-pack, slumped in the hall where he always chucked it. I ran upstairs and opened his door.

Ben was lying on the bed, his head on the blood-spattered pillow.

'What happened in here, Ma?' he asked languidly. 'Did someone commit suicide?'

FIFTEEN

'd said I'd try to get over to Mary Griffin's. And I'd said I'd sort out the return of Dodge's van. The presence in my house of a son with a driving licence offered a way of killing two birds with one stone.

Also, it ensured that, at least for the drive over to Ferring, Ben would not be on his own. I knew what he'd said about his bloodied bedclothes was a joke, but my son joking about suicide was never good news. Ben was in a bad way. Apart from any other signs, the fact that he'd turned up in Chichester during university term-time told me that.

So, I was kid-gloved with him on the way to Mary Griffin's. I told him briefly about her situation, just that she'd been a victim of domestic violence. And asked if he'd mind driving the Morris Tipper back to Dodge's. I told him Dodge was a bit debilitated at the moment, but I didn't tell him why.

Ben was delighted. I knew he would be. It had been the same with Oliver. When he was low, the prospect of a physical task, something that demanded no intellectual input, had always cheered him. At least, for a while.

'Riq and Raq animation project going all right?' I asked, sounding as casual as I could, as we drove out of Chichester on to the A27.

'Hit a bit of a brick wall there, Ma,' he replied. But his tone wasn't downcast. It was dangerously bouncy. 'I think maybe I need a little space from Riq and Raq.'

His use of the word 'space' offered me an obvious cue to ask about his relationship with Tracey. Too obvious. As if Ben had planted it there. Something he was quite capable of doing. So, I resisted asking him about Tracey. Let that conversation come in its own time.

'Dodge is in a bad way,' I said.

'I could see that from the state of my bed.'

'Yes. So, if there's anything he needs help with when you're there . . . you know, just moving stuff . . .'

'Of course I will, Ma.'

'And I'll come over and pick you up when I'm through with Mary.'

'Sure.'

Till we passed Arundel, there was silence in the Yeti. Not only silence, actually. There was also a large elephant. The elephant of the reason why Ben had come home so suddenly. And that elephant in the Yeti might well have been related to another elephant, also looming large – the situation regarding Tracey. Which in turn produced a third elephant, bigger than the other two – the state of my son's mental health.

Finally, the silence was broken. 'And how's your work, Ma? Any juicy murders?'

Ben had become rather more involved than I would have wished in my dealings with the case of the murder victim Kerry Tallis. I hesitated for a moment as to whether I should discuss Ingrid Richards with him. I have to be extremely strict about client confidentiality. But in this case, since Ingrid never got as far as being a client – and since she was dead – I could see no harm in talking about it to my son.

I gave him the briefest of résumés – how Alexandra had approached me, my meeting with Ingrid, the fact that Alexandra's father was Niall Connor.

'Niall Connor the journalist?' Ben asked.

My son's long had an interest in typography. I think, in an ideal world, that's where he'd like his career to develop. He once confided in me a long-held dream of one day inventing a definitive font, one to rival Helvetica or Times New Roman. As a result of this ambition, he has always collected newspapers – online, I'm glad to say, so I don't have a hoarding problem in the immediate family. He's not just interested in the fonts, though, he devours the content too. From his teenage years, Ben's always preferred reading newspapers and magazines to novels. So, I wasn't surprised that he knew about Niall Connor.

'Makes sense that those two would have got together.'

'Ingrid Richards and Niall Connor?'

'Yes. Birds of a feather. Both recklessly brave, just waiting for the next war to rush out to. Both highly successful. And competitive, I bet.'

He spoke with admiration. I wondered if there was an element of identification. I read that a lot of such characters were depressive, finding, rather in the manner of Graham Greene, that the adrenaline of physical danger allayed their mental anguish.

Anyway, because it was rarely that I could impress my children, I said, 'I actually had lunch with Niall Connor yesterday.'

'Did you?' Yes, Ben was impressed. 'Why?'

'He wanted to know what I'd thought of Ingrid Richards when I met her.'

'And what did you think, Ma?'

'I thought she was remarkable.'

'Hm.'

There was another silence. We turned off the A27 towards Worthing.

Then one of the elephants in the Yeti revealed itself. The big one.

'I'm not in a good place, Ma,' said Ben.

When he was in the Morris Tipper and about to leave from Mary Griffin's place, I couldn't stop myself from saying, 'Drive carefully.'

'Why?' he asked with sudden aggression. 'Do you think I'm about to drive this thing into a tree at high speed?'

'No, I just—'

'I'd never do that,' he said. Which reassured me.

'Not to Dodge's van,' he added. Which reassured me less. As with Oliver, there was a savage wit that emerged when Ben was depressed.

There was nothing I could do except let him go. What he'd said was true. When he was at his lowest, his respect for Dodge's van was considerably higher than his respect for himself. But, at that moment, there was no one I would rather he'd been going to see than Dodge.

The two of them both had their problems, but got on

surprisingly well. I doubted that they ever talked about mental health, but they sensed each other's vulnerability. And they cooperated well on physical tasks. At one point they had floated the idea of Ben using his artistic skills to paint some of Dodge's furniture. It hadn't happened, but it was something that might develop in the future. And something that I think they'd both find therapeutic.

Anyway, I had to put Ben's problems on one side for a while. And concentrate on those of Mary Griffin. I steeled myself as I approached her front door.

Inside the house, what was most upsetting was the state Amy was in. The little girl could not be insulated from her mother's hysteria and she had become infected by it.

A good half-hour was needed to bring the pair of them into something approaching calm. By then I'd managed to get Mary on to a sofa with a large mug of tea, and Amy on the floor playing with her replacement *Frozen* figurines. But the little girl wouldn't move far. She was constantly checking her mother was still there and clearly suspicious that I was about to spirit Mary away. Poor mite, I couldn't blame her for her paranoia. No way she could understand the details, but she certainly knew something unpleasant had happened.

'And there really is no one,' I asked, 'who you could leave her with, just while you recover?'

Mary shook her head. 'He made me cut off contact with all my friends.'

'Family?'

Another shake of the head. 'Wouldn't work. My mother would take Amy like a shot, but she'd spend all her time poisoning Amy's mind against Craig.'

Which, given the behaviour of the little girl's father, might by many people be seen as entirely reasonable. But I knew I couldn't say that.

'And the police . . .? There's no way you might—?'

Mary shook her head violently.

'But now if it can be proved that Craig set up the ex-con to—'

'No! If I went to the police, he would literally kill me.'

Hearing the incipient hysteria in her mother's voice, Amy looked up at her. The tiny bottom lip trembled. It wouldn't take much to tip her over the edge again.

'And you say,' asked Mary, 'that there's no danger of Dodge bringing charges?'

'No.' I said the word ruefully, but she sighed with relief. 'Incidentally, Mary, I'm sorry but I must ask this. There wasn't anything with Dodge, was there?'

'What do you mean?' she asked in complete innocence.

I spelled it out. 'Craig clearly thought there was something between you. Something sexual.'

'God, no. Me and Dodge? He's a lovely guy, but he's never come on to me or anything like that. He hasn't even looked me in the eye.'

'No, that's what I assumed, but I had to ask.'

'Yes. I don't think you understand Craig's jealousy, Ellen. Dodge was the one who suffered this time and I feel really guilty about that. But Craig would have reacted the same if the person coming to the house had been just making an Amazon delivery. He doesn't like me seeing other people. Any other people – particularly men.'

'I thought that was probably it.'

'It's his way of showing he loves me.' Her voice had taken on a pleading tone now. 'Like all the other terrible things Craig has done. They're all expressions of love.'

In the face of statements like that, it was difficult to know how I could help Mary Griffin.

My mobile rang on the way back to Dodge's at Walberton. I checked the display. Edward Finch.

I don't normally do work calls at the weekend, but there was something about the widower's strange behaviour that intrigued me. I parked on the side of the road and called him back.

'Ellen,' he said, 'I've been thinking about some of the things you said.'

'Oh? What in particular?'

'About letting go. About how I've got to let go of Pauline.'

'It's part of a process, Edward.'

'Yes, I understand that. But in fact, I'm talking about letting go of Pauline's possessions, not my memories of her.'

'Good.'

'You said I should get back in touch with you when I was ready to do that . . . get rid of the possessions, that is.'

'Yes.'

'Well, I'm ready, Ellen.'

I arrived at Walberton to find the van neatly parked outside. Which was a relief. When he's low, Ben can be dangerously unpredictable. The door to Dodge's live-in workshop was open. I tapped on it as I entered.

Inside, Dodge was lying on his home-made bed, his pillow propped up on the wooden structure like a bookrest. He had no covering over him. Even in the brief time since I'd last seen him that morning, his facial bruises had entered a new spectrum of colours. The plasters I'd put on had been replaced by some kind of green paste. At the antiquated range on which Dodge did his cooking, Ben was stirring a battered saucepan, taking instructions on how to mix some herbal remedy. The atmosphere between them was warm and relaxed.

'I've come to fetch my son,' I said, 'but if you'd rather we stayed . . .'

'No, it's fine,' Dodge croaked from the bed. 'He's been very helpful.'

'It's really cool, Ma,' said Ben. 'This natural healing stuff. Kind of makes more sense than getting into the clutches of Big Pharma.'

'I'm sure it does.'

'The multinationals are just after profit. They're capable of inventing diseases just so's they can sell people remedies for them.'

'Maybe.' I wasn't about to get into a discussion of pharmaceutical companies. I said honestly, 'I can't claim to know much about it.'

'You don't need to know anything about natural healing when you've got Dodge around. He is the Herbmeister.'

'I know.' I looked across at the figure on the bed. The sight still made me angry. How could one human being do that to another?

'Dodge, are you sure you don't want us to stay? I could cook us some lunch or . . .'

'No. Really. I'll be fine.' His words were distorted by his swollen lips. 'Just need time to heal.'

'Well, you will call me, won't you, if you need anything?'

''Course I will. And thanks, Ben, for acting as my nurse.'

'No worries. Glad to help.'

'Obviously, Dodge,' I said, 'if there's any heavy lifting that needs doing over the next few days, Ben'll be more than ready to help out.'

'Sure thing, mate,' said my son.

'Thanks, mate,' said Dodge. 'I'll be fine. Like I say, healing just needs time.'

Because of my recent encounter with Mary Griffin, I couldn't help saying. 'And you're absolutely certain that you don't want to report what happened to the police?'

'Never been more certain of anything, Ellen.'

It was rarely that Dodge used my name. The fact that he did seemed to reinforce his determination. I knew I couldn't sway him.

Ben followed Dodge's instructions as to where to put the potion he was brewing, and we were ready to leave.

'Hang on in there, mate,' said Dodge to my son.

I'm sure nothing had been said between them about the state of mind Ben was in, but Dodge instinctively empathized, understood.

SIXTEEN

I stopped at Sainsbury's on the way into Chichester, to buy the makings of Sunday lunch. If I'd been on my own, I would have had an omelette but, given the fact that I had a large son with me, I planned something more elaborate.

Some depressives lose their appetite when they're down. Ben never has. In that he's like Oliver. Oliver never lost his appetite for food. Or drink. Particularly drink. Ben's like him in that too. In so many ways he's like Oliver. That's why I worry so much about him. Can a child ever recover from the fact that his father committed suicide? Can the man's widow ever recover, come to that?

We agreed on steak for lunch. Didn't need to ask, really. Ben's always liked steak. Since he was about five, if there was a birthday meal coming up or some other celebration, he would demand, 'Steak and Mum's fat chips.' (That was before he'd developed the affectation of calling me 'Ma'.) He never wanted any other vegetables or garnish, just far too much ketchup. Ben's ultimate comfort food.

I'd got a couple of cases of Merlot at home, so we'd be all right for that, but I did also buy a new bottle of whisky. Famous Grouse, that's what Oliver always drank. OK, I've read all the medical stuff, I know alcohol's a depressant, but I also know my son. For Ben, before alcohol's a depressant it's a relaxant. And he's likely to be a lot more confiding and open with me when he's got a couple of Scotches inside him.

Anyway, it's once he's stopped drinking that he's likely to get depressed. There was no way I was going to let him out of my sight for the next few days.

As soon as we arrived back at the house, I got out one of the heavy-bottomed tumblers, put in three lumps of ice and handed Ben the opened bottle of whisky from the cupboard. I poured myself a glass of Merlot and started peeling the potatoes to make 'Mum's fat chips'. (No great secret about how I've always done them – I always use King Edwards and double-cook.)

I didn't initiate conversation, just waited till Ben came round to it. That happened when he'd finished his first Scotch and poured a second one. He began slowly, off the main subject that I knew he'd get round to in time. 'Dodge didn't say anything about how he got into that state . . . you know, who attacked him.'

'Well, that's Dodge for you.' A silence. 'Do you want me to tell you what happened?'

'Not really. Was it something to do with the domestic violence woman?'

'Yes, it was.'

'OK, that's fine. I don't need to know more than that. If Dodge didn't want to volunteer anything . . .'

The ice lumps clinked against the glass as he took another long swallow. Then he said, 'God, Ma, I am hopeless.'

I have a lot of experience of talking to depressed people and I know the worst thing is to immediately start trying to jolly them along. 'In what particular way?' I asked.

'Oh, I don't know. Every way. There doesn't seem to be any direction I can turn without hurting somebody.'

'Are you talking about someone specific that you're hurting?' There was no way I was going to bring the word 'Tracey' into the conversation. If he did, though, then fine.

Another silence. Another clink of ice. 'I just seem to cause trouble for everyone.'

'You don't cause trouble for me.'

'How can you say that, Ma? I can see how tense you are. You're watching me like you're terrified of what I'm going to do next.'

'Not terrified. Just concerned. I don't like seeing someone I love unhappy.'

'No? Well, you must've got used to it over the years, mustn't you?'

That was a deliberately hurtful remark. Ben rarely mentioned Oliver by name, but the implication was there.

'Things'd be better,' said Ben despairingly, 'if I wasn't here.'

'Here in Chichester?'

'Here anywhere. If there was no Ben Curtis in the world. It wouldn't matter. Nobody would notice. Be simpler all round.'

Again, don't argue. In this state, he's not going to be brought around by logic. 'How long have you been depressed, Ben?'

'All my life.' He flung out the answer.

'Yes, OK. But you know what I mean. This time. How long have you been this low?'

'I don't know. It feels like for ever.'

'And you have been taking the anti-depressants?'

'Oh yes. And how does that make me feel? Worse. I'm taking anti-depressants and I'm still depressed. They're useless. My last lifeline's gone.'

It was going to be a long day. I'd heard it all before, in virtually the same words, from Oliver. Many times.

Though it was May, I lit a fire in the sitting room. Comfort, comfort, comfort. Ben ate well, devouring the steak and 'Mum's fat chips'. He also sank a lot of Merlot. When we went through to the sitting room, he took the bottle with him. I did not object. So long as I was with him.

And I did not attempt to stem the familiar litany of self-hatred. Just listened, nodded, said 'Yes', and 'Mm'.

After about half an hour, he fell asleep in his armchair. He was clearly exhausted. I didn't know what time he'd got up that morning to make it from Nottingham to Chichester. Or maybe he'd travelled overnight. And if he was so depressed, the chances were that he hadn't been sleeping well for some time.

I looked at my son, his mouth sagging open, looking smaller than he really was, vulnerable. And I remembered how many times I had seen that vulnerable look, as a baby, as a toddler, small boy, teenager, student. He'd always looked as if he needed someone to sweep him up in their arms, to tell him things would be all right. It was a role I had always been happy to take on.

I was forcibly reminded, once again, how much I love my son.

I'd left the mobile in the kitchen, so fortunately it didn't wake Ben when it rang. I went through and answered. It was Alexandra Richards.

'Just wanted to say, nice to see you yesterday. Thanks for coming all the way over.'

'No problem. Good to see you too. And to meet Walt,' I added mendaciously.

'Yes. He's quite something, isn't he?'

I could think of no suitable answer to that, so I didn't offer one.

'I was just thinking, Ellen, there was something I forgot to tell you . . .'

'Oh?'

'. . . about the night Ingrid died.'

'Right.'

'Walt said I ought to tell you about it.'

'Fine.'

'And I do listen to what he says. He's full of good sense, you know.' Again, I had nothing to add, as Alexandra went on, 'I'm so lucky to have met him. I'd really given up hopes of anything ever happening on the romantic front.'

If I didn't say anything this time, it might sound as though I was endorsing her view of her unattractiveness. So, I managed to come up with, 'I'm so glad that you found each other.' Which is not the sort of cheesy remark I usually make.

Moving on, 'Anyway, Alexandra, what was it you were going to tell me?'

'All right. Well, the night Ingrid died, I said that I went to see her earlier in the evening.'

'Yes.'

'And I was probably with her about an hour.'

'Fine.'

'And I probably gave you the impression that I went home to Hastings straight after that.'

'I'm not sure you actually said it but that's what I'd assumed, yes.'

'Well, I didn't.'

'Go straight home?'

'No.'

When there's an obvious question to ask, I ask it. 'So, what did you do?'

'I stayed in my car, parked in Brunswick Square.'

'Why?'

'I was confused. I was always confused after I saw Ingrid. Here was this person who was my mother, to whom I owed a kind of duty of care, and yet I never knew whether she really cared for me at all. And the confusion was worse that day.'

'Why? What had made it worse?'

'It had been worse ever since Walt and I got together.'

'Ah. Was that because you hadn't told him of Ingrid's existence?'

'How do you know I hadn't?'

'Walt told me yesterday, while you were in the kitchen getting drinks.'

'I see. Once she was dead, I felt I could tell him. Up until then I didn't know. Our relationship was so new and fragile, I hardly dared believe it was happening. I wondered whether I could keep Walt in complete ignorance that I had a mother alive. I was afraid he might be scared off if he found out I was the daughter of a monster like that.'

I curbed my instinct to defend the late Ingrid Richards.

'So,' Alexandra went on, 'I just sat in the car trying to reconcile these conflicting thoughts and emotions.'

'How long did you stay there?'

'Till after midnight, just parked right outside Ingrid's block.'

'So, you could see who went in and out of the building?'

'Exactly, Ellen. That's what I wanted to tell you. In all the time I was there in the car, no one did go in or out of the building.'

I wondered for a moment why Alexandra had thought it necessary to tell me that. Of course, she didn't know how her father had stimulated my suspicion of her. Now, telling me she was almost definitely the last person to see her mother alive could only reinforce that suspicion. But then I reminded myself that she had been telling me on Walt's instructions. And only God knew what kind of power game he might be playing.

I was about to go back into the sitting room when my mobile's tone told me I'd received a text.

It read: 'We haven't met but I think you know who I am. My name's Tracey. Could we talk?'

SEVENTEEN

I doubt whether filling your son full of whisky and putting him to bed with an expired Zopiclone is recommended practice in most books of parenting. But that's what I did with Ben on the Sunday evening. As requested by Tracey, I didn't mention that she was in the area, staying with a schoolfriend near Worthing. Nor that she and I had fixed to meet the following day.

I also contacted Dodge again. He sounded in a bad way. Never one to make a fuss about anything, he did admit that he hadn't been able to get out of bed since we last saw him. His bruised body had stiffened up and, in spite of his various herbal remedies, he was in a lot of pain. I'm sure it was for that reason that he didn't raise objections to the plan I suggested for the next day.

Ben was bleary and uncommunicative the following morning. Probably the booze and the sleeping pill. But I did manage to get a cooked breakfast inside him. And quite a bit of black coffee, whose rehydrating effects, as they sometimes can, seemed to make him drunk again. He was almost giggly as I laid out my proposal for his day. But it was a dangerous, edgy kind of giggly. It had always been one of the danger signs when Oliver got like that.

First stop was Homebase to buy paint. I asked if he needed fine art stuff, but Ben said basic house paints would work better. Gloss. He chose the colours with care and got a set of different-sized brushes. He made only token objections to my paying. He agreed he was an impoverished student and I said I was investing in his future. (There was always in the back of my mind the fact that I had provided the deposit for Jools's flat in Herne Hill and I must at some point make an equivalent amount available to her brother.)

Then we drove to Dodge's. He looked terrible. The bruises

on his face and arms had found a whole new palette of colours. I made him some nettle tea before I left. I'd watched him often enough making it for me. And I'd brought a picnic lunch for the pair of them.

Making the furniture for Amy had not been a first for Dodge. He'd made stuff for children before – there was always a need for it in various charities. But, until the addition of the *Frozen* stickers, everything had been in plain wood. I'd suggested once or twice that maybe Ben could bring his skills to decorating the stuff, and Dodge had not ruled out the suggestion. But my son was rarely around in West Sussex, so the idea had never been followed through.

Till now. I thought it was the perfect short-term solution. Like his father's, Ben's gloomy introspection could be eased by having a project to get on with. A physical, practical project. And Dodge was in no condition to do anything for himself. I thought I'd devised a good mutual-aid scheme. Which might offer some stability at least until I'd talked to Tracey and hopefully got some idea of what was going on in my son's life.

But Tracey couldn't meet me till early afternoon, so I'd made a morning appointment to visit Edward Finch again.

The bungalow in Lancing looked extremely tidy. Whether that was due to the efforts of Edward or his long-suffering friend Cara, I had no means of knowing.

Even better, in the hall, neatly piled up against the wall, was a pile of boxes. They were new archive boxes, available from any stationery supplier. I was impressed by the fact that Edward had been organized enough to buy them. It suggested he was beginning to take the task of removing Pauline's clothes seriously. Very definitely, a step in the right direction.

He looked pleased, almost smug, as he saw me take in the pile of boxes.

'All her stuff in there?' I asked.

'Yes,' he said. 'Come and see.'

Ceremoniously, he led me through to the bedrooms. The first one, where he had been sleeping, was also much tidier than when I last saw it. So was the bathroom, which we had to go through to reach the master bedroom.

There, the transformation was complete. To demonstrate how totally he had fulfilled his brief, Edward had left the wardrobe and the dressing-table drawers open. Except for a clump of his clothes on hangers, pushed up to one end of the wardrobe rail, everything was empty.

'Well done,' I said, and I meant it.

'Yes,' he said with modest pride. 'It wasn't easy. But I managed it.' He looked around the room. 'And this no longer feels like Pauline's space.'

'That's good,' I said. 'You can keep your memories of her, without needing the constant prompt of her belongings.'

'Yes,' he said, almost dismissively. 'And also, of course, it means I can move on to the next stage of my life.'

'Exactly.'

He stood there, looking at me for a moment, and then said, 'You're a widow, aren't you?'

'How do you know that?'

'Cara told me.'

'Oh yes.' I'd forgotten I'd mentioned it, but now remembered her asking me. I'd thought it was rather a strange question at the time.

Edward continued to look at me. I felt slightly uncomfortable. Of what interest was my marital status – or lack of status – to him?

I moved almost brusquely through to the bathroom. 'I'll get that lot into the car. Then, when I get it home, I'll check through the stuff that has a resale value and take it to a charity shop in Chichester. You still don't want me to try to sell any of it for you?'

'No, no,' he assured me.

We were in the hall by now. 'If you wouldn't mind helping me, Edward, we'll get this lot into the car.'

'I wish you'd call me "Eddie",' he said, almost plaintively.

'All right, Eddie.' It seemed a small concession, given that I wasn't anticipating ever meeting him again. 'If you could just open the front door . . .'

The Yeti's boot is surprisingly capacious, and we got all of the boxes in with no problem. When the job was done, he lingered by his black front gate.

'I'll send you an invoice,' I said. 'At the rates we agreed.'
'Fine.'

'And I'd like to say: "Congratulations, Eddie." I know how hard it must've been for you to achieve what you have. And I hope that having made this enormous step will help you to come to terms with your loss.'

'Oh, that'll be all right,' he said casually.

'So,' I stretched out my hand to take his, 'good luck for the future.'

'Thank you.' He held my hand for a little longer than was necessary and seemed about to say something.

I didn't give him the chance. Extracting my hand, I said goodbye and got into the Yeti.

As I drove off, he still stood by the front gate, looking at me strangely.

For some reason, I didn't feel the appropriate sense of achievement. It should have been a case successfully concluded, an example of my skills as a declutterer helping a client come to terms with bereavement. But it didn't feel like that.

For the first time in a while, I found myself remembering Edward Finch's assertion that he had murdered his wife.

I didn't feel comfortable, anyway. But that was probably because I was nervous about my forthcoming encounter with my son's girlfriend . . . or maybe ex-girlfriend.

Giovanni, who runs Buon Caffè, knows I'll have a flat white and started making it as soon as I came through the door.

'How you doing?' he asked. 'Still sorting other people's rubbish?'

'Yes. You?'

'No. I've got enough rubbish of my own that still isn't sorted.'

It's an exchange we have, with slight variations, every time I go in the place. Fortunately, the weather was fine, one of those May days which feel like summer. So, I could sit outside, with a view of what used to be the Shippams Fish Paste factory. Depending on how the conversation ahead went, I might be better placed there than in the eavesdropping intimacy of the interior.

Tracey had described herself to me on the phone as 'long,

thin, with frizzy hair', and I had no difficulty in recognizing her as she approached.

She said, 'I knew it must be you.'

'Why, has Ben described me to you?'

'Not physically, no. But from what he's said about you, you fit the description.'

'I'm not sure whether I should be flattered or not.'

'Oh, you should be, definitely.'

Tracey was, as she'd promised, long and thin, and her dark brown hair was suitably frizzy. She had lively brown eyes and sparkly ear studs. Wore a grey hoody with the hood down, black jeans and white trainers. The jeans had splits at the knees which made me feel my age. I know, it's a generational thing, but I will never understand a fashion which actually makes people look shabby.

'Take a seat, anyway. Let me get you a coffee. What would you like?'

She asked for a flat white. Like me. I wondered if she was like me in other ways.

I gave the order to Giovanni. He said he'd bring it out.

Tracey and I sat opposite each other.

'You do know who I am, don't you?' she asked.

'I'd hardly be meeting you if I didn't, would I?'

'I didn't know. Ben can be so secretive at times. He's quite capable of denying that he's got a girlfriend, keeping my existence a secret.'

'Yes, he is,' I agreed. 'But you can reassure yourself, he has at least talked to me about your existence.'

'Good. I suppose.' She hesitated. Fortunately for her, at that moment Giovanni brought out the flat white. She took a sip and wiped any potential froth off her top lip (there wasn't any) before asking, 'What has he said about me?'

'Not as much as I would wish.'

That was possibly the wrong answer. It had the effect of making her anxious. 'What do you mean?'

'Sorry. I'm just naturally curious. All he's said is that he's been seeing someone called Tracey who is at Nottingham University – not Nottingham Trent – studying criminology. He hasn't told me anything else.'

'Typical Ben,' she said, which warmed me. It meant she knew a bit about how my son worked.

'And I've been a very good mum,' I said, 'not asking him for any more details. Waiting for him to volunteer some. Which I think could be a long wait.'

She chuckled, an encouraging sign, I thought, as I went on, 'So, I'm extremely glad to meet you.'

'Thanks.' Tracey took another sip of coffee and again wiped her upper lip, before saying despondently, 'I'm not sure that Ben and I are still seeing each other.'

'Oh.'

'That's why I've come down here. I want to know what's going on.'

'Did you have a row, back in Nottingham?'

She shook her head. The frizzy hair took a moment to settle. I was beginning to feel strong empathy towards her. This was a woman I could connect with. Now I was hoping that the relationship would continue.

'Not a row,' she replied. 'Ben doesn't do rows. He just goes quiet, doesn't look me in the eye.'

What she said was all remarkably familiar. It'd been just the same when Oliver descended into a black mood.

'And now I'm down here,' she went on, 'I sort of don't know why I've come.'

'To see Ben, presumably.'

'Only if he wants to see me.'

'Oh?'

'I've tried everything since we last spoke.'

'Which was when?'

'Saturday lunchtime.' I comforted myself that that was only two days ago. 'He'd agreed to meet up again.'

'You hadn't seen each other for a while?'

'Ben said he needs *space*.' That dreaded word. 'And, OK, because we're on different campuses, at different universities, it's easy enough to give each other space. But since then, each time I've tried to contact him, he's shut down on me. Won't answer his phone, won't reply to texts or email. He's cutting me off.'

She suddenly looked at me, with an expression of something

like horror. 'I shouldn't be talking to you. It feels like a total betrayal of Ben.'

'It would only be a betrayal,' I said, 'if one of us was trying to do him harm. And neither of us is. We both have the same thing at heart – Ben's welfare. His happiness.'

'Hm,' she said. 'Yes. I have a bit more at heart too, though.'

I was puzzled. I didn't know what she meant.

'Listen, Ellen,' she said. 'OK for me to call you Ellen?'

'Of course.'

'What I mean is, Ellen, that yes, I care about Ben's welfare. But I also care about my welfare.'

'So you should.' I wasn't sure where she was going with this.

'The fact is, I love Ben . . .' That was good to hear, though I was waiting for the 'but'. It came. 'But I find being with him sometimes can . . . I don't know . . . mess with my head.'

Now I could see where this was going. It was dispiritingly familiar.

'We have some great times together. Everything works.' She coloured, so I knew she meant the sex, but that wasn't the kind of thing you said to your boyfriend's mother. 'And nobody's ever made me laugh as much as Ben has.' I had used exactly the same words about Oliver.

'But' – I knew she was going to use the word again – 'then there are these times when he . . . just isn't there. I don't know where he goes' – I knew she wasn't talking about a physical absence – 'but it's not a good place and, even if I could go there with him, I wouldn't want to.'

'No,' I agreed.

'And I've been with Ben long enough,' she went on, 'to know that he does come out of that place. Eventually. It may take a long time, but he does come out. But while he's down, while he's in there, I feel terrible and I feel it's my fault.'

I had been in exactly the situation she was describing, but not for long. When I first saw Oliver depressed, I had blamed myself, thought I was doing something wrong, thought that it was me who was bringing him down. I hadn't spent time with anyone who behaved like that before. But then, after a while, I rationalized that he was a man suffering from an illness called depression. If I wanted to spend time with him, I'd just have to take on board that that was a part of the man I loved.

But how could I say that to Tracey? She was in her early twenties; she was finding her own identity. It would be desperately unfair for me to put pressure on her.

'And it messes with my head,' she repeated. 'It makes me feel inadequate, kind of sucks all the confidence out of me. I don't know what to do. Ben and I have a good patch and everything's fine. Then he goes into this dark place and it all falls apart. The we get back together and it's OK for . . . I don't know, a short while, and then . . . I don't know that I'm strong enough. Sometimes I think the most sensible thing I can do is just to walk away.'

Everything within me was screaming for her not to do that, but I knew I couldn't voice that thought. It would be unfair on the poor kid. This was something the two of them had to work out for themselves.

Instead, I said, 'You know by now that Ben suffers from depression, don't you?'

Tracey sighed. 'Yes, he's talked about it endlessly. It would be so much easier if it were a physical illness, something disabling, something that stopped him from, I don't know, getting upstairs or . . . That I think I could cope with. I've tried to understand what's going on with him but, never having suffered from depression myself, I find it difficult to get a handle on the condition.'

Again, she could have been echoing my own words. 'In Ben's case it's hereditary,' I said.

She looked at me in amazement. 'Surely not you?'

'No. His father.' A silence. 'Has he talked to you much about his father?'

'Hardly at all. Ben's said he's dead. That's all.'

Well, I wasn't about to tell her that Oliver had committed suicide, was I? That would have increased the pressure on her even more. If Ben wanted to volunteer the information, no doubt he would find the right time to do it. Though I was beginning to wonder how much more time he and Tracey would have together.

What she said next confirmed that anxiety. 'The thing is

. . .' Tracey began. She wasn't finding the conversation easy. 'The thing is . . . that all I wanted to be for Ben was a girl-friend. I do love him . . . but I didn't sign up to be a nurse . . . or a therapist . . . or a psychiatrist . . .' She winced. '. . . Or a mother.'

'He's already got one of those,' I said wryly.

'Yes. Yes, of course. I'm sorry if that sounded rude.'

'It didn't.'

'So . . . You won't tell him you've met me, will you?'

'If you don't want me to, I wouldn't dream of it.'

'OK. Well, Ellen, can you do this for me? Say to Ben that I've contacted you by phone – which is true – and that I told you he wasn't responding to my attempts to contact him.'

'All right.'

'If he wants to see me again, he must ring me . . . and we'll see where we stand.' She stood up. 'Now can I pay for the coffee?'

'Don't worry. I'll sort it.'

'Well, nice to have met you.'

'And you, Tracey.'

As she departed, her frizzy hair bouncing with the motion of her lithe body, I felt a huge respect for her. What she had done, actually meeting me face to face to voice her concerns about my son, must have taken a great deal of courage. But I also felt a huge sadness, because I didn't think I'd see her again.

Worse than that, I didn't think Ben would see her again either.

Things were good at Dodge's place. Ben had painted some great cartoons on a tiny desk that Dodge had made. It would make some child very happy. The style reminded me painfully of Oliver's work. Ben was pleased with what he'd done, and even more pleased that Dodge had commended it.

Dodge himself was up and about. Given the state of his bruises, I couldn't accurately state that he had more colour, but he was definitely in less pain. I didn't feel bad about leaving him on his own this time. It was left open as to whether Ben would go back to do more painting the next day.

In the Yeti on the way to Chichester, I told him that Tracey had contacted me, and spelled out her ultimatum.

Ben said nothing.

During the journey, my mobile rang. I didn't answer it while I was driving. Ben was too low to pass his usual comment on my old-fashioned distrust of technology.

I returned the call when I got back to the house. It was Detective Sergeant Unwin, the policewoman who had contacted me about the fire risk in Ingrid Richards' flat. Her tone was businesslike, but serious.

'I'm afraid I need to talk to you again, Mrs Curtis. There's been a new development in the case.'

EIGHTEEN

Ben didn't say whether he was going to contact Tracey or not and, though I felt a desperate urge to encourage him to do it, I knew I had to keep quiet. Nagging had never helped with Oliver either. Like his father, Ben had to come to a decision in his own way, in his own time. But that doesn't mean I found the waiting easy. With either of them.

When we got back to the house, he went straight upstairs, still not having spoken since we left Dodge's. I tried to persuade myself he wanted privacy to call Tracey, but I knew that wasn't it.

I went and did a bit of tidying-up in the kitchen and thought about what I'd cook us for supper. But I was really killing time until the police came.

Detective Sergeant Unwin had said it would be best if she and another officer came to the house. As soon as possible. Made me think that, with the 'new development', the case had become more serious.

Funny, from our first phone conversation, I'd pictured her as large and overbearing, but in the flesh Detective Sergeant Unwin was tiny, birdlike. Though that actually didn't stop her from being overbearing. Her sidekick, Detective Sergeant Gupta, was a good head taller, with short-cropped black hair. Neither was in uniform, but their similar black trouser suits made them look as if they were.

They both refused my offer of tea or coffee. They sat side by side on my sitting-room sofa, with me perched forward in an armchair opposite. I felt unreasonably nervous. Gupta had an iPad. She would be taking any notes that needed taking. It was clear from their body language that Unwin was the boss.

'Thank you very much for seeing us, Mrs Curtis,' she began.

It wasn't one of those 'Call me Ellen' moments, so I just said, 'No problem.'

'You were extremely helpful during our first conversation and there are a few details of what we discussed then that I'd like to explore further.'

'Fine.'

'I've explained to Detective Sergeant Gupta how you came to be involved with Ingrid Richards, how you were assessing the fire risk at her premises.'

That wasn't entirely accurate but not worth arguing about.

'I've also told her it was your view that the deceased was aware of the danger, but you thought she could manage the risk.'

Again, I could have taken issue about the detail but didn't.

'All of which would be fine,' Unwin continued, 'had the situation remained as it was when we last spoke. But we do now have different information. We have the results of the post-mortem on Ingrid Richards' body and they reveal that, as well as a lot of Jameson's whiskey, she had ingested sleeping pills that evening. Zopiclone, to be precise. The pathologist could not be certain but, from the residue found in her stomach, he got the impression that the pills had been ground up, presumably for ease of swallowing with a drink.

'Now, this news does rather change our perspective on the case.' She could say that again. My mind was instantly buzzing with new possibilities, but I didn't think it was the moment to say anything, as she went on, 'While it does not rule out accidental death, it does also open up the possibility of suicide . . . or even foul play.'

Detective Sergeant Unwin focused her small eyes on me. 'So, Mrs Curtis, when you visited Ingrid Richards, did she by any chance mention whether she was in the habit of using sleeping pills?'

No difficulty with my answer. 'She did actually bring up the subject, yes.'

'And what did she say?'

'She said that the life she'd led, the stress she'd been under in conflict zones throughout her adult life, meant that she could sleep anywhere. In fact, she said: "I've never had any need of sleeping pills."'

This brought a gasp from Detective Sergeant Gupta, followed

by a look of reproof from her senior. In the police force it was unprofessional to betray such instinctive reactions.

'You're absolutely sure about that, Mrs Curtis?' asked Unwin.

'Those were her exact words.'

'Hm. Interesting.' The two sergeants exchanged a look. 'Particularly interesting because Ingrid Richards' daughter told us this morning that her mother had been taking Zopiclone for years.'

Things didn't look good for Alexandra. What she had told me about staying in her car in Brunswick Square after seeing Ingrid on the evening of her death seemed deliberately to have ruled out the possibility of anyone else visiting. At least till after midnight.

And then Walt had volunteered, amongst a lot of other stuff that I really didn't want to know, that Alexandra had been a habitual user of sleeping pills. Zopiclone, to be precise. He had seen it as his duty to 'wean her off them', but that didn't mean she hadn't still got a supply.

Unwin had said they'd spoken to her 'this morning'. Where had that been, I wondered. On the phone? In Hastings? At a police station? And, as the case against Alexandra seemed to be building up, would she have been allowed to leave the police station?

I couldn't help remembering one of the first things Alexandra ever said to me. 'My mother's going to kill herself. If I don't kill her first.'

Was it possible that the boost of her new relationship with Walt had given her the confidence to remove the person who had so overshadowed her life? The person who had taken all the oxygen, eclipsed her own personality?

By bizarre synchronicity, just as these thoughts were going through my head, I had a call from Alexandra Richards.

I couldn't stop myself from asking, 'Where are you calling from?'

'Home. Hastings,' she replied on a note of bewilderment. I suppose it had been an odd question. She wasn't to know I'd been visualizing her in a police station under arrest for murder.

But her thoughts proved not to be a million miles away from mine. 'I'd been wondering if you'd heard from the police?' she asked.

'Yes. Detective Sergeant Unwin and Detective Sergeant Gupta came to see me. They've only just left.'

'They came to see me this morning.'

'At home?'

'Yes. What did they ask you, Ellen?'

The enquiry sounded excited but not paranoid. I didn't get the impression that Alexandra felt threatened by anything the police had said to her.

I told her that the sergeants had asked me about Ingrid's use of sleeping pills. I also reported what her mother had said on the subject.

To my surprise, this didn't seem to faze her. 'Oh, I'd always assumed she did take them. I thought it was a hereditary thing, sleeping badly. Something I'd got from her.'

Alexandra was full of contradictions. At one level, she seemed to have hated her mother. At another, she seemed desperate – as she had with the folder marked 'Alexandra' – for anything that implied some closeness between them.

'I presume,' I said, 'that the police asked you again about the events of that Tuesday evening, the night Ingrid died?'

'Oh yes, we went all through that.'

'Did you tell them about you staying in your car outside the flat till after midnight?'

'Yes, I did,' she replied blithely. 'They reckon I was prob- ably the last person to see her alive.'

Her tone suggested she didn't see how guilty that made her sound. Surely it was only a matter of time before the police came back to her with a more targeted interrogation?

'So, everything you told them was the truth?' I asked.

'Well . . .' she responded, almost coyly. 'Everything I told them was the truth. But I didn't tell the whole truth. There were some details that I didn't think they needed to know.'

'Oh?'

'For instance . . .' She sounded on the edge of schoolgirlish giggles as she said, 'I didn't tell them what I saw when I drove away from Brunswick Square that night.'

'So, what did you see?' I asked patiently.

'I had my headlights on full because there were no other cars on the road and, as I moved out of my parking space, I saw, only a couple of parking spaces away, Walt's car.'

'Really?'

'Yes. And he was sitting in it.'

'Do you know how long he'd been there?'

'No. But, needless to say, Ellen, I felt wonderful.'

'Why?'

'Because it showed how much he loved me.'

After the call had ended, I found myself wondering whether Alexandra could really be as naïve as she appeared to be. Didn't she realize that what she'd just told me placed Walt firmly in the frame as a suspect? She reckoned he'd followed her from Hastings to Brunswick Square because he didn't want her to have any secrets from him. He wanted to know who she was visiting there. She said at that stage he knew nothing about Ingrid's existence, so he was checking up on his girlfriend's movements to see if she was visiting another lover. She found that very flattering. And she considered it was a demonstration of his love.

My reading of the situation was that, although Alexandra hadn't mentioned Ingrid, Walt could easily have found out about her. He and Alexandra were cohabiting, for God's sake. I'd actually observed his lack of inhibition about going through her papers. There was bound to be something in the Hastings house that referenced Ingrid Richards.

A cynic – which I wasn't usually, though with Walt I was once again prepared to make an exception – a cynic might very quickly have put him on the list of potential murderers. I couldn't forget his claim to being 'someone who could sort out her problems with her mother, once and for all'.

I didn't think it would be long before Walt was on the police radar.

NINETEEN

That Monday evening, Ben went all quiet on me. He did come out of his room for supper, which he ate in complete silence. I knew better than to try and initiate conversation. He refused my offers of wine or whisky and went back up as soon as he'd finished. When I called after him, offering another expired Zopiclone, he didn't reply.

Probably because of that and a mind full of other things, I didn't sleep well. When I did finally get off, I woke up soon afterwards, trembling and sweating from a recurrent dream that hadn't troubled me for some months. Hadn't troubled me to the extent that I'd made the foolish assumption I was over it for good.

But no, the dream was back with its full, terrifying power. I'm seated, strapped in, one restraint tight across my stomach, the other diagonal, cutting a sharp line between my breasts. Even though I've had the dream so many times, I always start in ignorance. I don't know where I am or why I'm there. That only adds to the horror.

Then, gradually, in that strangely distorted timescale of dreams, I realize I'm in a car, locked in a garage. There's a mouth-drying smell of petrol. And then, as I try to counteract that with a gulp of fresh air, I suddenly know that what I'm breathing is not air. Not that mixture of nitrogen, oxygen, argon and other gases which sustains life. No, I'm inhaling something noxious, something that will choke me and cause every organ of my body to close down.

Every time, just before asphyxiation overcomes me, I wake up in a smothering twist of sweaty bedding.

And I wake knowing that, at moments of stress, I am doomed in dreams to relive the circumstances of Oliver's death for the rest of my life.

I felt terrible, but when I made it down to the kitchen on the Tuesday morning, Ben looked much worse than I did. He was fully dressed, and his hollowed eyes suggested he hadn't slept at all.

'I need to go back to Nottingham,' he said.

'You sure?'

'Yes, Ma. Got that "Riq and Raq" project to finish.'

'Of course.' There were a lot of questions I wanted to ask, but I stuck with: 'What do you want for breakfast?'

'Bacon and eggs, maybe? As you see, I've made coffee.'

'Yes.'

I cooked his order, bulking it up to a Full English. The least I could do was to see he went back to Nottingham well fed. I guess we did talk a bit over breakfast. He asked automatic questions about Fleur and Jools, but he wasn't listening to the answers.

I couldn't resist saying, 'You know, if you want to stay longer . . .'

'I know. Need to get back to face the things that need facing.'

I so wanted to ask if that meant facing Tracey, but I curbed the urge.

After he'd finished eating, I offered to run him down to the station.

'I'll walk it. Do me good.'

He went up for his backpack. I stood waiting for him, awkward in my own hall.

He didn't resist the big hug I gave him, but his body felt tense as coiled metal.

'I know there are lots of things you want to say, Ma, but I know what they are, so you don't need to say them.'

'Right. Well, can I just ask you to text me or something to say you've arrived safely in Nottingham?'

'I'm only going on a train, Ma. It's not an expedition up the Amazon.'

'I know, but . . .'

'I'll text you,' he conceded. 'Ma, I'll be OK.'

I wished I could believe him. And then he was gone.

I felt as if part of my body had been wrenched away.

I couldn't settle to anything that morning. There were things I felt I should be doing, like going to see Minnie, checking up on Dodge and Mary Griffin. I also needed to check through the clothes I'd taken from Edward Finch's bungalow and see which should be chucked and which should go to the charity shops. But everything seemed like too much effort. I kept trying to think what more I could have done for Ben. I felt inadequate as a mother, as a person.

And my mood wasn't lifted by a call from my mother.

'Ellen, I've just had a call from Kenneth.' Her husband. 'As he was driving into Chichester just now, he was sure he saw Ben.'

No point in denying it. 'Yes. He was down at the weekend.'

I knew what she was going to say so well that I could have joined in. 'You didn't tell me.'

'No, Fleur. It was spur of the moment on his part. I didn't know he was coming until he arrived.'

'Some crisis?'

That, too, was predictable. I'd never openly discussed Ben's mental health with my mother, but she'd somehow got an inkling of it. As she had with Oliver when I started seeing him. Back then she had thought my new boyfriend was 'unstable' and that I had taken a risk in marrying him. The wisdom of that opinion was, to her mind, vindicated by Oliver's suicide. These things were never said aloud between us, but the implication was always there. Perhaps it was part of her acting skill that made Fleur such a mistress of implication.

'No, I don't think so,' I lied. 'Just fancied seeing his old mum.'

'Didn't fancy seeing his grandmother,' she said, piqued. And absolutely in character for her not to repeat the word 'old'.

'He's under pressure with an animation project he has to deliver.'

'Oh yes?' she almost snorted. 'Well, fortunately, his sister is not so remiss in making contact. Have you heard from her recently?'

'Not for a while.'

'No, I thought not,' said Fleur with satisfaction. 'We had quite a long call on Sunday.'

'Good.'

'Nothing important. Just girlie chat, you know.'

'Mm. And she's all right?'

'Oh, absolutely fine. So busy. How she manages to cram in so many fashion shows and brand launches and . . . I just don't know. And her work as an influencer seems to be expanding too.'

'Good for her.'

'Oh yes. Funny, once we two get chatting, we could go on for hours. It's often the case, though, isn't it? That closeness in family relationships can skip a generation.'

This was deliberately offensive, but I was practised in not rising to such remarks. I let it pass.

'And of course, Jools reiterated her invitation for me to stay with her if I was up in London. Did I mention that to you?'

'You did, yes.'

'I don't suppose you fancy a spot of lunch at Goodwood . . .?'

'Thanks for the thought, Fleur, but I do have things to do. I am quite busy at the moment.'

'Of course,' she said. 'A cleaner's work is never done, eh?'

As I said, the call did not improve my mood.

And it did get me thinking about mother/daughter relationships. Which, of course, took me back to Ingrid and Alexandra. And, nearer home, my relationship with my own daughter.

'Hello?' Jools's voice sounded warm and welcoming.

'Hi, it's Ellen.' I don't know when I got into the habit of using my first name with my daughter, rather as I had with Fleur. I'd rather be 'Mum', but Jools somehow doesn't seem to like that. And she'd never called me 'Ma'. That was a kind of private joke between me and Ben.

'Oh.' The instant disappointment in her tone was not encouraging.

'Just rang to see how you are.'

'Fine. Fine.' Sounded reluctant to be talking to me. Rather be doing something else.

'Still busy in the fashion world?' As I said it, that sounded archaic to me. I wish I could share more up-to-date jargon with my daughter.

'Yeah, all going fine there too,' she said.

'Fleur told me you're becoming an influencer.' I tried to bleach the unfamiliar word of any intonation.

'That's the plan. I've done a few Instagram videos and stuff, but it takes a long time to build up the number of followers you need to make money from it.'

'I'm sure it does,' I said, already feeling a bit lost, even more detached from my daughter's world.

There was a silence, very brief but uncomfortably telling, before I said, 'And still going to lots of fashion shows and product launches?'

'Oh yes. Actually, I've got to be off for one shortly.'

My fault. I had given her a cue to duck out of the conversation. 'Oh, before you go, Jools.' Even now, my instinct was to say 'Juliet'. 'Have you heard anything from Ben?'

'No.' The tone of her reply made the question sound incongruous. How likely was it that she and her brother would be in touch? I still felt guilty about that. You keep reading and hearing of these families where siblings bond instinctively and never do anything without telling each other about it. Juliet and Ben got on fine when they were tiny but, come the teenage years . . . They were always totally different. Juliet very practical, a problem-solver, more like me, I suppose. She's got my colouring too. But Ben was always the dreamer. More like his father.

And when that father commits suicide . . . well, perhaps it's not the ideal scenario for family bonding.

'It's just,' I said, 'Ben was down for the weekend.'

'Oh yes. Was he throwing another wobbly?'

That was how Jools saw it, his mental illness. How she'd always seen it. Or claimed she'd always seen it. I think somewhere, deep down inside my daughter, there's an empathetic person fighting to get out, but she'd built such a hard shell around herself that it's a tough struggle.

'No, Ben was fine,' I lied. 'Did you know that he'd got a girlfriend?' I put it in the present tense, though I was rather afraid it might not be.

'Yes, I heard that.'

'From Ben?'

'From Fleur.'

That was predictable. 'Incidentally,' I said, 'Fleur's very chuffed that you've invited her to stay in the flat when she's in London.'

'Well, it's not a problem for me. There's plenty of space.' Realizing she'd inadvertently given herself a cue, Jools said, 'And, of course, if you were ever up in London and needed a bed . . .'

Rarely had an invitation sounded more reluctant. I contented myself with saying that the demands of SpaceWoman meant I was not often in London.

'All well with the flat?' I asked.

'Yes. Fine. And yes, Ellen,' she said wearily, as if by rote, 'I am very grateful to you for putting up the deposit so I could buy the place.'

Of course, that wasn't why I'd mentioned it. But Juliet always had been hypersensitive to anything she might interpret as criticism.

I knew I wasn't going to get any further in terms of rapprochement. That day. One day maybe . . .? I wasn't holding my breath.

'Anyway, you'd better get off to your fashion show or whatever it is.'

'Sure. Good to hear you, Ellen.'

'You too, Jools.'

I had cut out and kept the Ingrid Richards obituaries. I went back through them. I don't know what I was looking for but had the nagging feeling I was missing something.

The post-mortem findings showed that Ingrid Richards had ingested Zopiclone. Having lived with someone who was a suicide risk, I couldn't put her in the same category. Like me, Ingrid didn't have a self-harming bone in her body. Her energy and, yes, lust for life made such an outcome impossible. Which meant her death must have been murder.

Since I had first reached that conclusion, her daughter had been shaping up as the prime suspect. But now Alexandra herself had turned the spotlight on to her 'new man', Walt Rainbird.

His presence in Brunswick Square on the night of Ingrid's

death was, at the very least, surprising. From what Alexandra had said, she had not even mentioned her mother's existence to him. So, he must either have done some research through his girlfriend's papers, or possibly followed her car that evening from Hastings to Hove.

Walt was an arrogant little tick who prided himself on being able to sort out Alexandra's problems for her. But would he have gone as far as eradicating what he saw as her main problem, her mother? Did he perhaps have murderous bones in his body?

Before I pursued that line of enquiry, though, I wanted to find out more about Ingrid Richards' life and career. Hence the obituaries.

One detail which hadn't registered with me before was that Ingrid had come from a very wealthy family. Her father had made a great deal of money in property, buying cheap during World War II, and watching the profits accumulate thereafter. He'd died in the 1970s, though Ingrid's mother had survived till 2016. Ingrid was an only child, so presumably the legacy which Alexandra received was a considerable one. Why the money had skipped a generation and not gone to Ingrid herself, I don't know. Perhaps she had disapproved of how her father made his money and wanted nothing to do with it? Too independent to be funded by inheritance? She'd wanted everything she possessed to be the product of her own efforts?

Or maybe she had persuaded her mother to draw up a will that would fund her granddaughter for life? Thus freeing Ingrid to wash her hands of that responsibility? As she had, it must be said, washed her hands of many of her other maternal obligations.

No means of knowing. Pure speculation on my part.

The other thing that struck me for the first time from the obituaries was a coincidence of dates. Nineteen eighty-six. A lot of things seemed to have happened in 1986. It was then that Ingrid Richards and her cameraman Phil Dickie had been injured by shrapnel from the car bomb. It was also in 1986 that Niall Connor had achieved the career-changing coup of rescuing Paul McClennan from Hezbollah. Which placed both of Alexandra's parents in Beirut at the same time.

Was it stretching conjecture too far to think that might have been when their daughter had been conceived?

Alexandra herself might be able to confirm that but I didn't feel inclined to ring her. I hadn't yet sorted out in my head where she and Walt stood in the suspect stakes.

But, of course, there was one other person who had maybe witnessed events in Beirut in 1986. The cameraman, Phil Dickie.

I had no idea even whether he was still alive. None of Ingrid Richards' obituaries confirmed that, though the implication was that he'd certainly survived the injuries received from the car bomb. But there was no other reference to him. Phil Dickie seemed to have vanished off the radar. Though sharing the same risks, cameramen don't have the kind of profile that reporters do.

When it comes to tracking people down, there's probably never been a better time in human history. I started with social media. I'm not very keen on it as a concept, but I need a presence on Facebook and LinkedIn for professional reasons. SpaceWoman gets quite a lot of enquiries and bookings that way. Mind you, I've never posted anything personal. I only share my life with people I want to share it with. And, though I'm far from reclusive, there are few of those.

Several Philip Dickies listed on Facebook, but none fitted the profile. Though it was entirely possible that the cameraman had moved to Cincinnati or Rolleston, New Zealand, those two candidates were far too young to have been filming in Beirut in 1986.

So, I moved on from social media to a general search. As is so often the case when you go online, the initial results were not promising. The juxtaposition of the two words 'Philip' and 'Dickie' yielded a surprising number of the results about Lord 'Dickie' Mountbatten of Burma, uncle of Prince Philip.

Then I got entangled in a stream of references to the science-fiction writer, Philip K. Dick.

After a good few more false leads, I did eventually find something. 'Philip Dickie Family Films' said the website. It gave a studio address in Dorking, Surrey. The company offered a service converting cine film to DVD and other media.

'Preserve Those Memories and Play Them Back at Will with the Latest Technology.' They did editing, too. 'Package your Past into a Professional Standard Documentary to Delight Family and Friends.'

It wasn't a lot to go on, but at least it was related to film. Presumably, the technology had changed considerably from what a cameraman might have been using in 1986, but it was the kind of work that someone invalided out of more active filming might be able to do. It was worth a punt.

On the 'Contact' page of the website there was an email address and a mobile number. In my experience, people are much more likely to answer texts than emails. I sent one, reading: 'Please ring me about Ingrid Richards' death. I am not a journalist.' I gave my name but no reason for my interest in the case. If I was contacting the right Philip Dickie, he would either be intrigued and want to talk to me. Or, more likely, he wouldn't.

My little online excursion had only lasted half an hour. But at least it was half an hour when I wasn't worrying about Ben.

I cooked an omelette for lunch and in the afternoon forced myself to be more positive. The clothes which had belonged to Pauline Finch were still in the back of the Yeti. I got the boxes into my front room and went through them. One pile for recycling, the other for hardly worn stuff that could go to the charity shops.

There's quite a broad range of charity shops in a city like Chichester. It has more than its fair share of wealthy, well-meaning older women to staff them. Local prosperity also ensures that the quality of second-hand clothes available is remarkably high. Designer labels at knockdown prices. They do good business.

And, though I would never have told Edward Finch, his late wife's wardrobe wouldn't be of interest to the snootiest of the charity shops. Too much Marks & Spencer, Next and Country Casuals. Which is not my style either, though for different reasons. When I'm not wearing my blue SpaceWoman livery, I just slop around in jeans and T-shirts (much to the disgust of Fleur and, when she's around, my fashion-conscious daughter Jools).

Anyway, I'm an expert on the local charity shops. I have a lot of dealings with them and I know exactly what they will accept or reject. So, after a quick visit to the recycling bins, I targeted the right shops and offloaded the rest of the late Pauline Finch's wardrobe.

I was nearly home when the mobile pinged. I didn't check it till I was in the house, imagining Ben sending me up again about my unwillingness to use the phone in the car. It was a text from him, saying he was back in Nottingham. That's all it said, though.

I had one call that evening. I was hoping it would be Phil Dickie. It wasn't. The voice at the other end of the phone identified herself as 'Cara Reece, Eddie Finch's friend.'

I thought that, bar sending the invoice, my duty in that area was all done, but Cara said, 'I'm afraid Eddie's in trouble again.'

TWENTY

I didn't sleep well and faced the Wednesday morning blearily. Yes, it was mostly worry about Ben. But also trying to impose a pattern on the shattered jigsaw of ideas about Ingrid Richards' death and the possible involvement of Alexandra and Walt. The one person I didn't worry about in my wakefulness was Edward Finch.

But when I got up, though, I realized his was the one area of my troubled life where I could take some positive action. Cara's phone call had left me in no doubt that, like it or not, I had to pay another visit to the Lancing bungalow.

I have a kind of rule that, except in special circumstances, I don't make work calls until after nine thirty. I'm not interested in other people's morning routines, but I reckon that gives them long enough to have completed them. I'd call Edward later.

I found I was sitting in the kitchen over my second cup of coffee and feeling sorry for myself. Having witnessed depression first-hand from husband and son, I know I'm not a depressive. But that doesn't stop me from getting down. Non-depressives have a right to feel down too. The only difference is that when we feel down it's for a reason.

And I know, for me, the only way to get up again is to do something. Preferably something that involves helping someone else. It may sound pious but it's true – the best way to stop thinking about yourself is to think about others. Maybe I should embroider that on a sampler and hang it on a wall somewhere . . .?

I rang the care home and said I'd visit Minnie at ten.

She was getting weaker. It was sad to observe, every time I saw her, how much closer the skin was to the bone. And the sequence of strokes had left Minnie's movement severely impaired.

But she was remarkable. She still somehow managed to read. The local library was good at keeping her supplied with books – one of the librarians delivered them to the care home personally. And it went without saying, they were all about London.

As I had intended, the visit did have a therapeutic effect on me. On Minnie too, I hope. She made me think, as I sometimes do, of the randomness of death. Here was an old woman I didn't know very well, but whose company I enjoyed. And, probably within a few months, she would no longer be around. I wouldn't feel exactly grief or bereavement, as I would with a close friend or a family member, just a sense of absence. Why did Minnie have to die?

On the plus side, I left the care home that day knowing that 'to walk penniless in Mark Lane' meant to have been swindled. That 'bunny' once meant 'talk' in Cockney rhyming slang, apparently from 'rabbit and pork'. Which sounded pretty dubious to me, but then I would never argue with Minnie's sources. I also discovered that a 'kingsman' was an outsized coloured handkerchief worn by costermongers. Though I couldn't think there'd be many occasions when that would come up in conversation.

Back in the Yeti, I took out my mobile. I knew I had to ring Edward Finch but felt unaccountably unwilling to do so. Probably because I desperately wanted to ring Ben, but I knew I shouldn't. Mustn't be a suffocating mother, must wait for him to contact me. Wait for him to volunteer what – if anything – was happening with Tracey.

To distract myself again from Ben, I tried to think of something I could do to further what I increasingly saw as my 'investigation' into Ingrid Richards' death.

It struck me that I could ring Walt, inform him what Alexandra had told me about his presence in Brunswick Square on the relevant evening. I didn't have a phone number but recalled him proudly naming his company as 'Walter Rainbird Computing Solutions'. I found the website, rather scruffily put together, I thought, for someone advertising his computer skills. A distinctly amateur look to it, far too many fonts being used in the display. There was a mobile number. I left a message, asking him to call me.

Then, reluctantly, I rang Edward Finch.

He had that look on his face that I'd seen before. The schoolboy who had broken the rules but felt rather proud of having broken the rules.

'I'm afraid I've backslid,' Edward said when he opened the front door.

'Show me,' I said, quite sharply. I don't like people messing me around and, until I had proof to the contrary, that's what Edward Finch seemed to be doing.

'Ooh, Ellen,' he said coyly, 'you're very masterful. Or should that be "mistressful"?'

In no mood for that kind of banter, I pushed past him towards the master bedroom. There was nothing lying on the bed or the floor. I opened the wardrobe.

Four new dresses were hanging there. All Marks & Spencer. Remarkably similar to some of the ones I had so scrupulously removed.

'You bought these?'

He nodded sheepishly.

'Why?'

Edward Finch had a speech prepared to answer that question. 'I could say the reason I bought them was that I couldn't manage without something that reminded me of Pauline. If you'd known the garments were here and asked me on the phone why I'd bought them, that's what I would have said. But that's not what I'll say now you're actually here.'

'Why should it make any difference whether I'm on the phone or here?' He was playing some game of his own and I was quickly losing patience with it.

'Because I wanted you to come here,' he said mysteriously.

'Did you? And, incidentally, why wasn't it you who rang me yesterday? Why did the call come from your friend Cara?'

'I thought you'd be more likely to come if it came from Cara. She would make it sound as if I were in genuine need. That way you wouldn't have been fighting your feelings.'

'I beg your pardon?' Edward Finch now seemed to be moving into the outer reaches of sanity.

He then said, unbelievably, 'You don't have to pretend with me, Ellen.'

'What?'

'You know, from the first moment we met, there was something between us.'

It takes a lot to render me speechless, but that did it.

'Don't deny your feelings, Ellen. You love me and I love you.'

That I had not been prepared for. I mean, since I've been widowed, I've experienced a good few . . . what shall I call them? Well, to sanitize the reality, let's say 'romantic over-tures'. I've fought off the predictable local gropers. And the male halves of couples who I reckoned Oliver and I knew as friends, but who reckoned I, as a widow, must be 'gasping for it'. They're, incidentally, not friends any more.

I'd never say that Oliver was the only man I'll ever love. Unlike my mother, I am not prone to making dramatic state-ments like that. But I do think it's unlikely that I'll ever get into another relationship like that with a man. Certainly not a cohabiting relationship. I don't say that out of self-pity, I'm just being realistic. In my fifties, I've got out of the habit of that kind of love. I don't miss it. I miss Oliver himself every day, but that's different.

And friends say, 'Oh, you'll be surprised. When the right person comes along . . .'

I don't think I'd have the emotional energy.

But none of that had prepared me for a come-on from a little creep like Edward Finch. Or for what he said next. 'You're about the same size as Pauline was, Ellen. Those dresses would fit you. Do you want to put one on now?'

As if what he'd said wasn't offensive enough, he then had the nerve to put his arms round me.

I'm not a habitual slapper. No, perhaps I should rephrase that, could be misinterpreted . . . I don't often slap people. Certainly not clients. In fact, I disapprove of any kind of violence against another human being. But for Edward Finch, I was prepared to make an exception. I lashed out with my right hand and caught him hard across the cheek. The mark reddened instantly.

He had the nerve to smile and say, 'Don't fight it, Ellen. You know you really want me. And you really want to put on one of those dresses.'

'What I really want,' I said, 'is to leave this place and never see you again!'

'You say that, but you don't mean it.'

'Thank you, Edward, but I do know exactly what I mean. And I mean to have nothing more to do with you, beyond sending you an invoice for the time of mine that you've already wasted.'

'Time with the one you love is never wasted. You'll come round, Ellen.'

I marched to the bedroom door. Then had a thought, stopped, and looked back at him. 'Tell me something.'

'Anything you want, my love.'

I winced at the endearment, but said, 'When we first met, you suggested to me that you had murdered your wife.'

'Yes.'

'Though you hadn't, had you?'

'No,' he admitted.

'Then why the hell did you say it?'

'I wasn't so sure of you then, Ellen. I wanted to be certain you'd come back again. I thought you'd be intrigued, knowing I had a dark side.'

I left the bungalow, slamming the front door behind me.

And found Cara Reece waiting by the garden gate.

'You've seen Eddie?' she asked.

'Yes.'

'And is it true, what he told me?'

'I don't know what he told you,' I said curtly, 'so I don't know whether it's true or not.'

'Eddie said you were going to get married.'

'Me? To him? You've got to be joking.'

'So you're not?'

'No! He lives in a fantasy world.'

'Yes,' said Cara. 'Eddie's a very unusual man.'

'That is certainly true.'

She must have registered the irony in my words, but she didn't seem upset. Rather the reverse. 'I was rather worried,' she said. 'About you and him.'

'Why?'

'Well, I was friends with Eddie and Pauline . . . you know, all being schoolteachers and . . . but I never really liked Pauline. It was Eddie I liked. And now Pauline's gone . . . I enjoy doing things for Eddie.'

'He's very lucky to have you,' I said, not adding that he took her for granted and treated her with contempt.

'Yes. And I'm so lucky to have him . . . I mean, now I know he hasn't got you.'

He never had me! I suppressed the urge to say the words out loud. If Cara Reece wanted to continue being patronized and treated like a doormat by Edward Finch . . . well, that was up to her. It was clear that she got some perverse satisfaction out of the relationship. Fine by me.

So long as I didn't have to have anything more to do with him.

'And actually,' Cara said rather winsomely, 'I'm about the same size as Pauline. And you. The new dresses would fit me.'

I shuddered, said goodbye to her and got into the Yeti.

My mobile rang while I was still driving through the bungaloid sprawl of Lancing. I parked and answered it.

'Is that Ellen Curtis?' the voice at the other end asked cautiously.

'Yes.'

'You left a message for me. I'm Phil Dickie.'

I felt a surge of excitement.

'Hello.'

'Hi.' He still sounded guarded. 'Your message said you're not a journalist.'

'I'm not.'

'Then why are you interested in Ingrid Richards' death?'

TWENTY-ONE

'They didn't understand so much about PTSD back then.'
Phil Dickie was sitting in his studio in a special chair. It had a complex arrangement of padding, presumably to ease the pressure on his back injuries. A pair of crutches was propped up against his desk. He wore a polo shirt and, incongruously, shorts. I say 'incongruously' because they revealed that one of his legs was made of articulated metal. The trainer at the end of it matched the one on his real foot.

He saw where I was looking and grinned. Whatever the state of the rest of his body, he had a very handsome face. Startlingly blue eyes, short white hair, neatly trimmed white beard. Probably in his mid-sixties, a good decade younger than Ingrid Richards.

'Sorry,' he said. 'If I know I'm going to see people I put on a pair of jeans. Today I just thought I'd be editing in here.'

'I gather from your website that you digitize old cine film.'

'Yes. That's how I started after . . . you know, when I could think about working again. There was a whole generation of people with yards and yards of cine, family holidays, birthday parties, you know the kind of stuff . . . which they could only watch by setting up projectors and what-have-you. And they wanted that transferred into a form that could be watched on their computers. So, I set up the business. I don't do so much of that digitizing now. More family documentaries.'

'Which are . . .?'

'Sort of tributes to individuals who're not famous. Say, a couple coming up for their Golden Wedding . . . their kids want to get together a montage of old photos, bits of video, memories from family and friends talking straight to camera. They give me the stuff, I edit it all together, make a nice neat little package.'

'I should think they're very popular.'

'Increasingly, I'm glad to say, from a business point of view. And there'll be more to come with the next generation, the ones who grew up photographing everything on their mobile phones. There'll be no lack of footage then. Though quite a few tend to do their own editing now. They've got the technology to do it on their phones. But a lot of them're so cack-handed, or so bloody lazy, I think my services will still be required. I'll have enough work to see me out.'

Phil Dickie grinned ruefully. 'Once I'd recovered from my injuries . . . well, no, I should say, "Once I'd come to terms with my injuries . . .", I looked around and thought, "What can I do now?" There was no way I could go back to being a news cameraman. Hadn't got the mobility, apart from anything else. And also . . . when I started getting flashbacks from the PTSD . . . well, I wasn't that keen on putting myself back into a war zone.

'So, I'd got a bit of money. Though I was freelance, the BBC did give me some compensation because I was injured while working for them. I put the money into this studio and set up my film transfer business. It was never going to recapture the excitement of what I used to do, but it was something. And I needed some kind of income to see me through the rest of my life.'

His lips twisted into a grimly sardonic expression. 'Better than nothing, eh?' he said.

'So how old were you . . . when it happened?'

'Out in Beirut? Thirty-three. Doing the job I loved. Recently married. Thinking of trying for a baby.'

'And are you still . . .?'

Another sceptical twist of the lips. 'No. I'm afraid my wife decided she didn't want to be married to a bomb site. That wasn't what she'd signed up for.'

I was inevitably reminded of what Tracey had said about her relationship with Ben.

'She got married to someone else soon after. Three kids they've got.'

I didn't say anything. There wasn't anything suitable to say.

'So here I am.' Phil Dickie looked bleakly around his domain. The desk he sat at was a landscape of switches, dials, buttons, and faders. In front of him, an internal window opened on to the small, unlit recording studio.

'Sorry. Enough about me,' he said. 'You wanted to talk about Ingrid Richards.'

'Yes. Do you mind?'

'No. Since I've heard she's dead, I've wanted to talk to someone about her. But I've lost touch with all my old contacts in that world. Deliberately lost touch with them, in most cases. But now I do need to talk about her.'

I asked, 'Is that why you agreed to see me?'

'I suppose that was part of it, yes. And particularly because you said you weren't a journalist.'

'Am I right in deducing you don't like journalists?'

'I like individual journalists. I liked Ingrid Richards. A lot. That is why I'm talking to you.'

'But journalists as a breed?'

'I used to like them. Used to spend a lot of time drinking with them in the watering holes of various war zones. The Commodore and the Pickwick in Beirut. But after I got injured, I lost my taste for the company of journalists.'

'They hounded you?'

'That's a very well-chosen word, Ellen. "Hounded." Yes, that's what they did. I was in a pretty bad state emotionally. And all they wanted to talk about was the one thing I didn't want to be reminded of.'

'The car bomb?'

'Exactly. God, they were persistent. I thought their interest was rather ghoulish.'

'So, you never talked to any of them about what had happened?'

'I talked to one. From one of the tabloids, can't remember which. When I saw what he wrote about me, I swore I'd never talk to another journalist.'

'Had he got the facts wrong?'

'Not that. I wouldn't have minded that. No, it was the way he made me come across. As pitiful. And that's the one thing I have never wanted to be. OK, maybe life dealt me a pretty lousy hand, but the last thing I want from anyone is pity!'

The recollection had made him angry. I didn't blame him.

I'd felt the same after Oliver's death. I didn't mind people showing empathy. But pity? No way.

He continued, 'Sorry, going off on one there. Let's get back to Ingrid. That's who you want to talk about. I want to talk about her too. We lost touch completely after . . . But I always thought our paths would cross again at some point. Now, of course, they won't . . . and I feel . . . kind of . . . Like I say, I want to talk about her. Incidentally, that was a pretty sad way for her to die, wasn't it? In a fire in her flat. A domestic bloody accident? The Ingrid Richards I knew may have been many things, but she was never careless about her personal safety. Still, maybe as she got older, the marbles may have got shaken about a bit and—'

'She still had all her wits about her, Phil.'

'Ah. So, are you implying that her death might not have been an accident?'

'There are people of that opinion,' I replied judiciously.

'Really?' He was silent for a moment as he took in the implications of that. 'How long had you known her, Ellen?'

'Only met her the once.' And I gave him a quick résumé of my professional involvement through Alexandra.

'Yes, I did hear Ingrid had a daughter.' Phil Dickie scratched his beard thoughtfully. 'I remember being gobsmacked when I heard that. So out of character. I couldn't see the Ingrid I knew interrupting her career to have a baby.'

'Well, she did. Do you know who the father was?'

He shook his head.

'Niall Connor,' I said.

'Bloody hell!' He really was taken aback by that.

'Did you know him?'

'Yes. Not well. But I spent some evenings drinking with him and a bunch of other correspondents in the bar at the Commodore. He was a bit of a Jack-the-Lad, always chatting up the birds' – he coloured – 'as we used to call them back then. Probably not allowed to say that these days. Offend someone, no doubt.'

'Might offend birds?' I suggested.

'Hm. All I know is that everything I say seems to offend someone these days. But Niall . . . Niall and Ingrid . . .' He shook his head in bewilderment. 'That's a match-up I'd never had considered in my wildest dreams.'

'Presumably,' I said, 'you didn't see much of Ingrid in the months after you were both injured?'

'Didn't see much of anyone. Or anything. I was put into an induced coma out in Beirut, then flown back to Brize Norton. In and out of various military hospitals over the next eighteen months, having operation after operation. Not a lifestyle conducive to keeping in touch with people.'

'You don't know how long Ingrid was hospitalized, do you?'

He shook his head. 'Not as long as me, that's for sure. I heard from someone it was only a couple of months. Maybe three or four. She wasn't as severely injured as I was. I suppose that's my claim to fame. I put my body between Ingrid Richards and the car bomb, so I took most of the shrapnel. How bloody heroic.' He let out a bitter laugh. 'Be more heroic if I'd done it deliberately, though, wouldn't it?'

'Mm.' I was following another line of thought. 'I was just wondering . . . if Ingrid was unconscious for some months in hospital, when she did come round and find out she was pregnant, it might have been too late for her to have an abortion.'

That would tie in with what Ingrid had said to me about her pregnancy with Alexandra and why she wasn't aborted. 'Circumstances meant that that was not an option.' Such circumstances might well have been being treated in hospital for shrapnel wounds.

The cameraman shrugged his shoulders at my suggestion. 'That's possible. I'm afraid I don't know. I was totally out of it at the time.'

'So, Phil,' I asked, 'do you literally remember nothing from when the car bomb detonated to when you woke up in an English hospital?'

'I do remember the moment of impact,' he said, 'and a bit after that. I think it was a time before I passed out. There was a sort of moment of shock before I felt the pain from the shrapnel wounds to the back of my legs, and my back and . . . everywhere.'

'You weren't wearing body armour?'

'No, we were slacker about that stuff back then. Cameras were heavier too. I found it much easier to carry and manipulate mine without being weighed down with body armour.'

'What about Ingrid?'

'She was wearing it. BBC were quite strict about people in vision wearing all the appropriate kit. And in Ingrid's case, well, I think it was part of her image actually, the way the Great British viewing public liked to see her. In her body armour, with the strap of her leather satchel across the front. That was what they paid their licence fee for, and she played up to their expectations.'

'Yes. I remember her doing news reports like that. It was quite a potent image. She looked totally fearless.'

'Oh yes. Of course, she wasn't. Nobody was. We were all shit-scared most of the time. But you got better at hiding the fear. Every day you survived, you felt, well, maybe I can cope with another day. The drink helped too.'

'And that famous leather satchel of Ingrid's?' I asked. 'What did she keep in it?'

'Everything.' The cameraman shrugged. 'Nowadays, of course, it'd all be electronic stuff – mobile phone, satellite phone, laptop, tablet, whatever. You forget how primitive the technology was back then. No mobile phones in the 1980s, no laptops. Very primitive metal detectors. Satellite communications, yes, but not very portable. Telex – God, telex was used a lot. Ingrid favoured old-fashioned spiral-bound notebooks. That was the archetypal image of the Press – intrepid reporter scribbling away in a notebook. Like Tintin and all the others.'

'So . . . going back to the car bomb . . . I'm sorry if that's painful . . .'

'It's OK. I can cope.'

'When the thing went off, you're saying that Ingrid was partly protected by the body armour?'

'Yes. Except for her face, of course.'

I had a vivid image of the deep dent I had seen in her forehead. It must have bled a lot when it happened.

Phil went on, 'Like I said, the reporters were encouraged to wear body armour if they were going to be in vision. Made them look as if they were taking responsible precautions . . .

though what constituted responsible precautions in a war zone was a matter of considerable debate.'

'Ingrid was going to be in vision at that moment? Were you actually filming her when the bomb went off?'

'We were setting up to film. Ingrid was about to do a piece to camera.'

'What about?'

'About one of the hostages who was being held out there. I don't know if you remember, but there was a journalist called—'

'Paul McClennan,' I interrupted, beginning to see where all this might be leading.

'Yes. Ingrid was very excited. She'd somehow managed to make contact with his captors. She had some deal going on with them.'

'Deal?'

'I don't know exactly what it was. Maybe get an interview with one of the men holding him? Maybe actually get an interview with Paul McClennan himself. That would have been television gold-dust. And the militias were getting increasingly canny about media manipulation. You remember all those videos they circulated? Hostages with copies of newspapers with dates on them? Hostages spelling out their abductors' demands. It was only a short step from that to one of the hostages actually being interviewed. And if there was any reporter out there capable of getting that kind of coup, Ingrid was the one. As I say, she was really excited about something that day. Kept telling me that all the details, passwords, maps and what-have-you, were in the leather satchel.'

There was a silence while I took in the implications of this. Then, very gently, I said to Phil Dickie, 'Look, I'm sure you don't want to be taken back to that moment, but would you mind telling me exactly what happened when the car bomb detonated?'

He rubbed a hand hard against his forehead, as if he could somehow erase the memory. 'I'm sorry,' he said. 'I should be over this now. We are talking more than thirty years ago.'

'If you'd rather not talk about it . . .' I offered him an exit, hoping to God he wouldn't take it.

Fortunately, he didn't. But even the thought of that time brought a glisten of sweat to his forehead. 'What do you want to know?' he asked.

'The moment the bomb went off, you were standing facing Ingrid, about to film her piece to camera – right?'

He nodded.

'Then – what? The blast knocked you over.'

'Yes, sent me smashing forwards. Fortunately, I was too far away actually to fall on to Ingrid. But, as I went down, I saw the shrapnel hit her forehead, saw this fountain of blood come spurting out. She fell like a stone. I was worried she was dead.'

'So, you were still conscious at this point?'

'Yes.'

'Do you think Ingrid was?'

'No.'

'Did you see anything else before you passed out?'

'Yes. There were people rushing around, though I heard them rather than saw them. People running away from the site of the bomb, people coming to help the victims. Total chaos.'

'Nobody came to help you?'

'Not then, no.'

'So, what did you see?'

He seemed about to say something, then checked himself. 'I don't know,' he answered slowly. 'Like I say, it was all confusion. I remember my last thought before passing out was – seeing the amount of blood she was covered in – that Ingrid was dead.'

'I see.'

'Mind you, I thought I was dead too,' said Phil Dickie. His expression turned very grim. 'Sometimes think it might have been better if I had been.'

TWENTY-TWO

'd managed to find a parking space directly outside Phil Dickie's studio and, when I got back into the Yeti, I checked my voicemail. There was a message from Alexandra Richards. I rang her.

'Have the police been in touch with you?' she asked immediately.

'Not since you and I talked on Monday,' I replied.

'They've just been to see me.'

'Ah. Unwin and Gupta again?'

'Yes. They asked if I'd ever used sleeping pills.'

'Really?' To my mind, the detectives had been rather slow in getting to that question. 'So, what did you say?'

'Well, I couldn't deny it. If they'd got a search warrant, they would have found packets of Zopiclone in my bathroom cabinet.'

'I thought Walt had made you stop taking them?'

'He keeps telling me to manage without them, and I am trying. But I like still to have a supply there, in case . . . you know.'

'Yes.'

'Unwin and Gupta took the Zopiclone. They put the packets in an evidence bag.'

'Ah.'

'That doesn't sound good, does it?'

'I'm not sure. It depends on what they think the Zopiclone would be evidence of.' I may have sounded a bit dense, but I didn't want to push Alexandra into saying anything that she wasn't ready to volunteer.

'There's only one thing they could be thinking,' she said quite logically. 'That the Zopiclone ground up in Ingrid's whiskey had come from this house.'

I was glad she had said it rather than me.

'But Unwin and Gupta,' I asked, 'didn't talk about anyone being charged with murder, did they?'

'No. They didn't talk about it, but surely the implication was there, wasn't it?

I was glad she'd taken the implication on board. Alexandra Richards was naïve, but she wasn't *that* naïve.

'Oh, I wish Walt was here.' There was a note of desperation in her voice. 'He'd know what I should do.'

'Where is he?' I asked, remembering I'd left a message for him to call me.

'He's out on a call, fixing someone's laptop in St Leonards. Oh, life is sometimes very difficult, isn't it, Ellen?'

I wasn't about to argue with that, but I wondered where the question was leading.

'You know,' she went on, 'when you have to keep secrets because you love someone.'

'You mean when that someone has asked you to keep something secret?'

'Yes. Exactly that.'

I could imagine quite a few things that Walt might have asked her to keep secret but, though I asked her very directly, Alexandra wouldn't tell me any more.

Before we finished the conversation, I did say – sounding rather pious, I'm afraid, 'All I would advise is that you don't start lying to the police. That's only going to create trouble for you.'

'I know,' she said miserably.

No sooner had I switched my mobile off than it rang. Synchronicity. Walt returning my call.

'What did you want to talk to me about?' He sounded as cocky as ever and I was amazed how quickly my dislike for him could be reignited.

'I wanted to talk about the night Ingrid Richards died.'

'Oh yes?' He didn't sound surprised. 'Have you talked to Ally about it?'

'I have.'

'So, you know I was in Brunswick Square that night?'

'Yes. But I don't know why you were.'

'Ah. Well, you know Ally and me are, like, "an item"?'

I could visualize him putting mimed quotation marks round

the words. Suppressing an inward 'Yuck', I replied, 'Yes, I had pieced that together. You've mentioned it enough times.'

He didn't seem aware of the edge on my remark, as he went on, 'I have discovered, over the years, Ellen, that what's really important in a relationship' – oh yes, like you're the guru of relationships – 'is complete honesty. No secrets from each other.'

Why, when I would have agreed completely with the principle put forward by someone else, did I feel so inclined to disagree with Walt Rainbird voicing it? I restrained the instinct.

'And,' he pontificated on, 'I feel that is particularly true when you're starting out on a new relationship. Complete honesty is essential.'

Again, I didn't argue.

'I have learned, from bitter experience, that any other approach can be very painful and destructive.'

'Bitter experience?' I echoed.

'Yes. In a previous relationship, I had the misfortune – well, I say "misfortune" but the outcome was fortunate – to discover that my partner was cheating on me.'

'Oh?'

'With someone else.'

That was another detail I could have pieced together for myself, but I didn't say anything.

'And it became clear to me, after some weeks of Ally and myself being "an item", that there was an area of her life that she was keeping secret from me. I refer to her visits to Hove.'

'Ah.'

'At least, at first I didn't know it was Hove she was visiting.'

'No?'

'She claimed that these unexplained absences were for meetings about this charity she's involved in. Bloody donkeys. She's obsessed with bloody donkeys. I think that's an area of her life that may need some changes. I'm not sure that I want a girlfriend of mine to be involved in a donkey sanctuary when—'

'Could we get back to her visits to Hove?'

'Very well. I must confess I was suspicious. About these charity meetings. It seemed to me strange to have charity meetings during the evening. And I'm afraid, after my previous bitter experience, the idea that Ally was cheating on me developed and, kind of, festered in my mind. I gave her the opportunity to offer an alternative explanation of what she was doing, but she stuck to her story which, increasingly, I knew to be false. So, one evening, when she said she was going off to one of her charity meetings, I followed her in my car.'

'This is before the night when Ingrid Richards died?'

'No, no, it was before that. So, I followed her and, once I was in Hove, I saw which building Ally went into and I'm afraid I put the worst possible construction on what she might be doing there.'

'You thought she was seeing another man?'

'I did. As I said, bitter experience. Once bitten, et cetera. I didn't stay. I drove straight back to Hastings. But when Ally got back that evening, I challenged her, and she persisted with the lie about the charity meeting. So, I decided to take more positive action.'

'What were you going to do?'

'Next time she went to Hove, I would once again follow her, but this time I would go into the building after her and find out who it was she was seeing.'

'So, you met Ingrid?'

'No, I didn't. I got delayed by some roadworks on the way from Hastings. Round Polegate it was. Ally's car had just gone through when the light went red. By the time I got through, I had lost sight of her. Then I took a wrong turning and got to Hove . . . I don't know, probably some quarter of an hour after Ally did. And, in fact, when I got there, she was just leaving the building in Brunswick Square.'

'So, you must have realized that, if she had been going there for a sexual encounter, it was just a quickie?' I suggested.

'That was not my immediate thought,' Walt said rather grumpily.

'So, did you stop Alexandra then and ask her what she had been doing?'

'No. I waited to see what she would do next.'

'And what did she do next?

'Ally got straight into her car and drove off . . . drove, I later discovered, straight back to Hastings.'

'So, did you follow her?'

'No.'

'Why not?'

'I thought I'd watch the building, see who came in and out.'

'Trying to spot your rival?'

'Something like that.'

'And did you see him?'

'No. I should have trusted Ally. But, as I say, bitter experience. I was possibly a little bit hypersensitive and paranoid.'

I would have said that was something of an understatement. 'So, when did you leave to go back to Hastings?' I asked.

'Round midnight.'

'And you had it out with Alexandra then?'

'No. I didn't go back to her place.'

'What?'

'I still have a flat of my own. In St Leonards. I went back there.'

'Why?'

'I was still angry with Ally. For keeping secrets from me. I wanted to make her suffer.'

You nasty little tick, I thought. Not for the first time.

'But then,' he went on, 'the next morning, Ally texted me. Told me her mother – the mother I didn't know she had – had died. Then, obviously, we met up again, and she explained everything.'

'And now you know about Ingrid's existence, the fact that she had a mother, why do you think Alexandra didn't tell you about her earlier?'

'I think she thought it might affect the purity of our love.'

'I beg your pardon?' I said, in a state of wince.

'Everything was so perfect. Ally and I had found each other. I don't think she wanted our happiness to be clouded by the presence of the woman who had made her whole life a total misery.'

'I see.' I wondered again whether it was more a case of Alexandra not wanting her mother to see what a creep she'd ended up with. But, as I had many times during this conversation, I kept my reactions to myself. My lip was beginning to feel the pain of being constantly bitten.

I did ask, though, why Walt had taken the trouble to call me back.

'You left a message. Simple politeness,' he said smugly.

'Surely there was more to it than that?'

'Well . . . Ally texted me to say the police had been in touch with her. She sounded worried. I thought you might know what they're up to.'

'Whether they're suspicious of her, you mean?'

'Yes.'

'If they are, you can easily stop that, can't you?'

'How do you mean?'

He really wasn't very bright. I spelled it out for him, 'The fire that killed Ingrid Richards started – or was started – late on the Tuesday evening or in the early hours of the Wednesday. You witnessed Alexandra leaving Brunswick Square . . . what time? Before eight, anyway.'

'Yes.'

'So, all you have to do is to tell the police that. I'm sure Alexandra has got the number for Unwin and Gupta, and she'll be off the hook.'

'Yes,' Walt said. 'Yes, I can do that for Ally. Set her mind at rest.' Instantly casting himself as the knight errant rescuing the damsel in distress.

'You said, incidentally,' I continued, 'that you didn't see your rival coming out of the building in Brunswick Square?'

'No,' he admitted.

I couldn't stop myself from saying, 'Which was hardly surprising, given that he didn't exist. But, more interestingly, did you see anyone else enter or leave the building?'

And Walt Rainbird finally told me something that almost justified his existence on this planet.

Having finished the two telephone calls, I was still, of course, parked in Dorking. I started the Yeti to drive back to Chichester.

But I was stopped by a tap on the window. Phil Dickie, on his crutches, was alongside me. I opened the window.

'I saw through the window that you were still out here,'

he said. 'Were you planning to make a return visit to the studio?'

'No. Sorry. Just doing a couple of phone calls.'

'That's serendipitous perhaps.'

'Oh?'

'Well, I was thinking, after you left, of something I didn't tell you . . . about when the car bomb went off in Beirut . . . about Ingrid.'

'What didn't you tell me?'

And Phil Dickie revealed something that, along with what I'd heard from Walt, made a whole lot of details fall into place.

TWENTY-THREE

I t was dark by the time I left Dorking. And I didn't go towards Chichester. There are times when being on one's own, with no kids or pets or husbands living at home, is a positive advantage. I was now so emotionally caught up the mystery of Ingrid Richards' death that I knew I had to go straight up to London.

And I would have gone straight up to London but for a road crash, which didn't, I'm glad to say, involve me and the Yeti. The only damage done was to my plans for the evening. I'd decided, foolishly, to go on the M25. Driven from Dorking to Leatherhead and got on to the motorway with no problem. I was just congratulating myself on how little traffic there was when everything ground to a halt. Absolutely solid.

Walt Rainbird had suffered a delay at Polegate of a quarter of an hour. Mine, near Leatherhead, took rather longer.

I checked the AA Traffic News on my phone and discovered there had been a 'major incident' on the M25 clockwise just before Junction 10. Never found out the details, whether anyone had been killed or injured. All I know is that I sat in the Yeti, unmoving, with the same car in front of me, the same one behind and the same ones either side, for over three hours.

By the time the traffic started moving again, it was far too late for me proceed with the rather vague plans I'd made for the evening. I would have to stay somewhere in London and reschedule for the morning. But where?

Then I remembered a flat in Herne Hill, for which I had paid the deposit. And the slightly ungracious invitation I'd had to stay there, if ever I was in London. I rang my daughter's number.

I hadn't been to the flat much since Jools moved in. A lot the first few weekends, helping her shift stuff around, even doing a bit of decorating. But since then, rarely. As I said, the demands of SpaceWoman, Chichester friends – and Fleur, of course – meant that I was rarely in London.

Also, to be honest, the place was too full of memories of Oliver for me to feel completely relaxed there. When we first got together, I moved into his houseboat on Regent's Canal and we enjoyed London to the full. Pubs, restaurants, movies, theatre, the lot. As a cartoonist for daily newspapers, Oliver knew some wild friends from the world of journalism and we had a lot of fun, liberally marinated in alcohol. He was still at the stage where he thought alcohol helped allay the depression. Actually, coming to think of it, he never progressed from that stage.

The arrival of Juliet curtailed our – well, certainly my – social life a bit, and when she started toddling around, living on a canal boat became impractical and dangerous.

That was when, in the face of strong opposition and uncertainty from Oliver, we had moved down to the South Coast. First, we'd had a big house in Funtington, then the current one a few miles away in Chichester. The second move was, of course, without Oliver. I couldn't face staying in the house in whose garage he had asphyxiated himself. When house-hunting in Chichester, I ruled out anywhere that had a garage.

So, for me, London was a bit like the Funtington house, a place of happy memories, shadowed and soured by subsequent events.

I was quite surprised when Jools said she wanted to buy a flat. Not surprised that she wanted to, but surprised that she reckoned she could afford to pay a mortgage. And, indeed, that in her early twenties she wanted to tie herself down with one.

But I shouldn't have worried. Shouldn't have been surprised either, come to that. Juliet had always had a good financial brain. Even when she was tiny, she saved her pocket money for things she wanted and only bought them when she'd accumulated the full sum. Never turned to Oliver or me to help her out.

Because of that history, she was embarrassed about asking me to help with the flat deposit. It was just a private arrangement, but she had worked out a repayment schedule and, so far, she's paid what she owes each month. She knows I wouldn't make a fuss if she didn't, but my Jools takes financial matters seriously.

Which is why I'm constantly amazed that she works in the fashion industry. Not the high-end, designer-label part of the business, but down the cheap end. The clothes she writes about, the ones she goes to product launches for, the ones she would like to promote as an influencer, are all cheapo garments, designed to be worn once or twice and then chucked away.

I'm not fanatical about green issues but, doing what I do, I've become increasingly aware of the importance of recycling. Spending time with Dodge has reinforced that belief too. So, having a daughter working in an industry which encourages a 'wear once and chuck into landfill' attitude is . . . well, at the very least, strange.

And, given the relationship that Jools and I have, I sometimes wonder whether she has chosen that sort of work just to annoy me.

Mothers and daughters, eh? I qualify in both categories and I still can't work it out.

When I'd got through on the phone to Jools, I had been surprised that she sounded positively benign. I wouldn't go as far as saying 'welcoming' but at least not downright adversarial. When I arrived at the flat, I discovered the explanation. She was pissed.

Not aggressively pissed, benignly pissed. Thank God. She'd been to the launch of some new online fashion magazine and clearly had a good time. She'd met some of the editorial staff and thought there was a good chance of her getting some work for them.

The fact that I have never read any of my daughter's fashion journalism might be seen as yet another example of bad parenting. But I have asked on many occasions to see in print or be given an online link to her writing and always received the same rebuff. 'No, Ellen, it's not the kind of stuff that would interest you.'

When I arrived at the flat, frazzled after my long traffic jam,

I found Jools had been benign enough to have opened a nice bottle of Cabernet Sauvignon and already poured me a generous slug. I was so desperate after the hours that I'd spent in the car that the first thing I had to do was fly to the loo. But when I returned, I took a grateful slurp of the red.

It was only then that I took in what my daughter was wearing. I'm not that old, but Jools's choice of clothes sometimes makes me feel very, very old. Jurassic old, at least. I know in my youth I wore some fairly ridiculous ensembles, but I think back then we did have a concept of things *going together*. Well, that was out the window so far as Jools was concerned.

That evening, for the event she'd just returned from, she had favoured leggings in a swirl of what would once have been called 'psychedelic' colours, a short shocking-pink lacy skirt and a blue PVC gilet over a yellow rugby shirt. Her feet were in silver trainers studded with purple sequins. Her make-up was a homage to the Addams Family. To complete the effect, her hair was gathered into two buns on top of her head, giving her the silhouette of Minnie Mouse.

What was terrifying about it, for me, was that what she was wearing must actually have been fashionable. Jools wouldn't be seen dead in anything less. God, I felt even older.

I knew my duty as a mother, though, and made no comment on her appearance. To praise it would have been recognized as duplicity, and to criticize it would have just confirmed her view of me as a fashion basket-case. I was quite glad I was still in my SpaceWoman blue polo shirt and leggings. Wearing my work clothes offered no opportunities for adverse comment on my sartorial choices.

'Have you eaten?' Jools asked.

'No.' I couldn't remember when any food had last passed my lips. Breakfast, maybe?

'Well, I don't cook,' said my daughter, stabbing another knifepoint into a traditional mother's heart, 'and I haven't got the energy to go out, so I'll order a Just Eat.'

'Fine.' I was still slightly shaken by the information that she didn't cook. I had taught her enough recipes during her teens to survive in a kitchen. Now apparently unnecessary. Another feature of her throwaway lifestyle.

'I fancy Mexican,' she said. 'You all right with that?'

'Sounds good.' I couldn't claim to have eaten much Mexican, but what I'd had I'd liked. 'You order for me.'

She did the business. For the first time, I took in the flat's interior. Starkly minimal but well done. Furniture a bit bony for my taste but more comfortable than it looked.

'Oh, incidentally, Jools, I wasn't expecting to be in London, so I haven't got any overnight stuff. Can you find me something to sleep in . . . and maybe a pair of clean knickers for the morning?'

'Sure, Ellen. No prob.'

'And what – will I sleep in the spare room?'

'No, you sleep in my room. I'll be in here.'

'Are you sure?'

'Yes. This thing we're sitting on opens out. It's a sofa bed.'

'So, what about the spare room? What happens there? Have you got a lodger?'

'No.' And then my daughter added gnomically, 'I don't use the spare room as a spare room.'

The food was good. Jools knew her way around a Mexican menu much better than I did. We were both so hungry that we hardly spoke till we'd finished the last refried bean. We'd finished the bottle of Cabinet Sauvignon, too, and Jools suggested moving on to gin. Pink gin with Fever-Tree tonic. As I said, I rarely drink spirits and felt that my daughter had probably had enough already that evening, but there was no way I was going to break the atmosphere between us by going into bossy mother mode.

Mm. I'd forgotten just how nice a gin and tonic could be. I felt more relaxed with my daughter than I had . . . well, since her father died.

Did I dare mention Oliver's name, I wondered. I didn't want to threaten this unprecedented moment of harmony, but I desperately needed to talk to Jools about him. And I think she needed to talk about him too.

I had no desire to be devious, but I still approached the subject in a roundabout way. 'At the weekend, Ben was talking about an animation project he's doing as part of his course.'

'Ah. Right.' She didn't sound particularly interested in her brother's doings, but mellow and unguarded.

'It's based on "Riq and Raq".'

'Ah.' No intonation at all.

'You know, it's a cartoon strip your father used to do.' Well, that particular elephant in the room had been referred to. It was a step.

'I've heard of the strip,' said Jools. 'Don't think I've ever seen any of them.'

'I've got quite a few of the originals in the attic at home. I think I might get some more of them framed . . . you know, like the "Major Cock-Ups" and "Teddy Blair" stuff that I've hung in the hall.'

It had taken me a long time after Oliver's death to reach the point where I could look at his work. Getting a couple of the cartoons framed and putting them on show in the hall had not been easy, but it had felt like an important step in my transition into widowhood.

The only reaction Jools gave was an almost imperceptible shrug. Then suddenly she looked at me. 'You're not suggesting I should put some of his cartoons up here, are you?'

'No, of course not.'

'Good. Because they wouldn't go with my stuff.'

'I can see that.' Enough of this circling round. I'd go for the direct approach. 'You never talk about him.'

'Nope.' She finished her drink and poured more. Just gin this time.

'I know it's difficult.'

'That's an excellent choice of word, Ellen.'

'I've found talking about Oliver makes it easier for me.'

'Well, I've found,' she snapped back, 'that not talking about him makes it easier for me!'

She was beside me on the sofa bed. I could see tears were pouring down her cheeks. Instinctively, I put my arms around her, as I had so often until she became a teenager. She didn't resist.

'You've shut in so much,' I said.

'I find that easier too,' Jools said, through tears.

'It's natural. Something unpleasant happens – something

unbelievably, cruelly unpleasant – and you try to shut it out. And why? Because the feelings are too powerful if you do think about it?'

My daughter didn't respond.

'Juliet – sorry, Jools – after Oliver died, I went through every kind of emotion, some I didn't want to acknowledge. Anger being a predominant one. I felt so furious with Oliver. Furious for his selfishness. Not for what he'd done to himself but for what he'd done to us. Oh yes, of course I knew that depression was a disease, that he couldn't help it, he was ill, but that didn't stop me blaming him. It wasn't a worthy emotion, but it was a necessary one. Is that the kind of feeling you're trying to shut out? Anger? Blind fury?'

'No,' said Jools through the sobs, so quietly I could hardly hear her. 'It's not anger. It's guilt.'

'Guilt? Why on earth should you feel guilt?'

'I think I, kind of, shut Daddy out.'

To an extent, I could see where she was coming from. Oliver had adored Juliet from the moment she was born. He'd loved playing with her. Often, when I thought he was up in his study drawing, I'd find him downstairs with her in a rubble of Lego. She was his beautiful little daughter, and he got an enormous charge from just having her around. They were amazingly cuddly with each other. Like many fathers who work from home, he got a real dose of Empty Nest Syndrome when Juliet started school.

But that was as nothing to what Oliver felt when she hit her teens. Suddenly there was this complex, spotty young woman who had periods and shrugged off her father's attempts to give her a hug. She was just behaving like any young girl of her age would, but for Oliver it felt like rejection.

And that development coincided with a fall in demand for his work as a cartoonist. Like many freelances, Oliver had always been paranoid about the prospect of the work drying up. And back then, to his mind, that was what was happening. Some fifteen years older than me, he felt that his professional life was over. And so, yes, at one level, Juliet's behaviour towards him had contributed to his depressive mood.

I didn't realize that she'd been aware of that. And the idea

that she had been bottling up this guilt for more than a decade
. . . it was a painful thought.

'Daddy was ill,' I said to her. 'I've felt regret about things
I could have done, the fact that I was out at the time he finally
decided to do it, but I really haven't felt guilt. I think I helped
him. He would have done it earlier, if he hadn't got the structure of a family around him, if he hadn't got people who loved
him and were still there when he emerged from the black
moods. I think I gave him a bit of stability. Not enough, but
a bit. And you did too.'

'Did I?' she asked, desperately clutching at any available
comfort.

'Yes, you did. He loved you. That didn't change. It was just
that the hatred for himself became stronger than the love he
felt for us.'

'Hm.'

There was a moment of stasis, the two of us on the sofa
bed, my arms around my daughter. One of the buns on top of
her head felt strange pressing against my cheek.

Then, abruptly, Jools moved away. 'I'm not normally soppy
like this,' she said. 'It's the booze. And I'm pre-menstrual.'

'It doesn't matter why. I'm glad we've talked about it.'

'Huh.' The brittleness had returned to her tone. 'I'll get you
some night things. There's a new toothbrush in the bathroom
cabinet.'

I had a fleeting thought that she might keep such a thing
for someone she brought back to the flat to stay over, but I
didn't pursue it. Like so many areas of her life, Jools's relationship history was a closed book to me.

'Incidentally,' she asked, 'will you tell Fleur we've had this
talk?'

'My instinct would be not to.'

'Good. She'd just blather on and on about it and say how
you shouldn't have married Daddy in the first place.'

That was a spot-on assessment of my mother's likely
behaviour, but I was surprised that Jools would voice it. I
didn't think I'd ever before heard her criticize Fleur.

'She is very grateful for the relationship she has with you,
Jools.'

'Fleur? Oh, she's easy. I just feed her vanity. It's easier to be someone else with Fleur than it is to be me with anyone.'

'Including me?' I asked, foolishly fishing for something positive after our recent rapprochement.

'Particularly you. I always have to be someone else with you,' said my daughter, instantly shutting the door to future intimacies. 'Anyway, I must get to bed. Got an early meeting in the morning.'

She moved brusquely round the room, clearly wanting me out of it so she could pull out the sofa bed.

'Yes, I've got quite a day tomorrow,' I said. Which was possibly an understatement.

Jools didn't ask what the day ahead held for me. She didn't talk about anything other than practical details of where I'd find towels and so on. She seemed ashamed of having let her guard slip. Maybe she did know how much it had meant to me, but she made no further reference to her lapse.

And there was no hug or kiss as we went to our separate bedrooms.

It took me a long time to go to sleep. Partly perhaps the unfamiliar bed, Herne Hill's different traffic noises from those of Chichester.

Also, I kept thinking about the tiny glimmer of hope that had been opened up in my relationship with my daughter. I knew I mustn't overinflate it – her reversion to the standoffish Jools at the end of the evening told me that – but at least, very briefly, it had been proved that we could communicate.

But probably the biggest factor in my sleeplessness was the prospect of the next day's confrontation.

As is so often the annoying case with a bad night, I ended up oversleeping my usual waking time. When I got up, there was no sign of Jools. A note on the kitchen table reading: 'See ya'. Just that.

I didn't feel hungry, so all I had by way of breakfast was a flat white, made in Jools's very swish Italian coffee-maker. Again, I found myself wondering about her sources of income. She certainly seemed able to live in some style.

I thought I'd better get out as soon as possible. The Yeti had ended up in a marked parking space the night before, but it might be in danger of an early morning ticket from some assiduous traffic warden.

Before I left, though, I paused outside Jools's spare-room door.

She hadn't said I wasn't to go in. And, having provided the deposit for the flat, I did feel some kind of proprietorial rights in the place. The door wasn't locked. I opened it.

The room was absolutely full of clothes. Hanging from wheeled racks. All new clothes, maybe worn once, undoubtedly freebies Jools had accumulated from all her fashion launches.

And none of them built to last. They reminded me again of that statistic about how 300,000 tonnes of garments are burnt or buried in the UK every year.

Why they were there, I could not imagine. Did my daughter make extra cash from selling them? Did she think she'd wear them all again at some point? Or was she curating an archive of instant fashion to be gazed at in disbelief by future generations? Hanging in her spare room, at least they weren't being burnt or buried. That was a small comfort.

But I couldn't dispel the idea that maybe I'd got a hoarding problem nearer to home than I'd previously thought.

TWENTY-FOUR

'd rung ahead, using the number on their mutual card, so I was expected in Primrose Hill. The house was Victorian and imposing, less than half the size of the Petworth one but, given London prices, worth many multiples of it. Two big-name journalists, all the columns and articles and books, plenty of money coming in.

Niall Connor opened the door to me. There was a rueful expression on his face, but also impudence. He looked at me with the assurance of a man who thought himself unfailingly magnetic to women. As he had in Petworth, he took it for granted that I was attracted to him. I couldn't help remembering Ingrid's comment that at his age the need for Viagra might limit the scope of a 'predatory pouncer'.

'Come through to the sitting room,' he said.

It was at the front of the house. Grace Bellamy was sitting there, with elegant coffee essentials laid out on a low table in front of her. The décor was, of course, exquisite, ready to be photographed for colour supplements and design magazines. Which I'm sure it had been many times.

Grace was, once again, dressed to complement her stylish surroundings. Definitely London clothes rather than country clothes. Niall, once again, went for shabbier chic. Jeans, a mauve cashmere sweater draped with studied abandon over a subtly frayed blue and white striped Oxford shirt. Still no socks underneath his brown leather slip-ons.

'You remember Grace?' he said.

'Of course.'

'And you said you wanted to talk to me about Ingrid Richards' death?'

'Yes. You did ask me to let you know if I heard anything else of relevance to it.'

'Absolutely, Ellen. And I'm very grateful to you for coming

here to tell me.' He brushed his forelock back with a practised, boyish air. 'So, what have you heard?'

'When we last met,' I began, 'we established that you knew Ingrid was writing a memoir.'

'Yes. She crammed a lot into her life. But' – he spread his hands wide in a gesture of philosophical resignation – 'Ingrid Richards' memoir is a work which now, sadly, the world will never see.'

'True. And, Niall, were you worried about the possible contents of that memoir?'

'Why should I be?'

'You and Ingrid, as well as being close at times, were basically rivals. Together in a variety of war zones, in competition for getting the best stories.'

'I don't deny that. Back then, we were all in competition with each other, Ingrid and any number of other correspondents. Yes, we played many games of one-upmanship. That was part of the fun of what we were doing.'

'And did you ever use underhand means to prevent a rival reporter from getting a story?'

'"Underhand"? That's a rather strange word to use in a journalistic context. Yes, of course we'd withhold our sources from other reporters. If one of us got a contact who promised to be useful, we wouldn't tell all the others about him. We might even send a fellow correspondent in the opposite direction from where we knew the action was going to be. We were all looking for exclusives. But I'm not sure that qualifies as "underhand". The history of journalism is full of such behaviour.'

'Might you try to queer the pitch of another journalist by giving them false information?'

'Of course we would. That was part of the game. Go for the scoop yourself and then put the other journos off the scent. Everyone was doing it. We had some unchanging rules of behaviour, the basic one being: "Don't make stuff up." Other than that, there were no rules. Everyone knew the score. But again, "underhand" is far too judgmental a word for what was going on.'

'I can't help noticing, Ellen,' said Grace, charming as ever, 'that, though all this is very interesting, it doesn't seem to have much to do with Ingrid Richards' death.'

'I'm getting there,' I said.

'Good,' she said, in a rather schoolmistressy tone.

'I was asking Niall about Ingrid's memoir, because I wanted to know whether he might be worried about anything she might write in it.'

He smiled blandly. 'My back is broad. Criticism is an essential part of the journalist's work. You can't please all the people all of the time. And, if Ingrid had scores to settle with me' – he shrugged – 'then let her write about them. No skin off my nose.'

'No? I want to ask you about the events of 1986.'

'Fine by me. An important year in my life, perhaps the most important year.'

'Of course,' I said. 'The year your daughter was born, apart from anything else.'

He gave a mock wince and Grace, I noticed, pursed her lips ever so slightly. 'Yes,' he said, 'though it was not until some years later that I knew of her existence. And I'm not going to pretend that it was news I welcomed. I don't think her mother did, either.'

That possibly confirmed my conjecture that Ingrid, hospitalized by her shrapnel injuries, had not realized she was pregnant until it was too late for an abortion.

Niall continued, 'Call me callous and unpaternal if you like, but I'm not going to pretend that, for me, Alex's appearance was the most important event of that year.' He affected an expression of boredom. 'Do you want me once again to go through the whole story of Paul McClennan's escape from his captors?'

'No. I know all the details of that.'

'Good. Then you will understand that springing a hostage in Beirut was probably the high spot of 1986 for me.'

'Yes.' Time to change tack. 'Niall, do you know who I mean when I say the name Phil Dickie?'

'Of course I do. Had a good few late-night drinking sessions with him at the Commodore. He was the cameraman with Ingrid when she was injured by the car bomb in Beirut.'

'Yes. He was injured too.'

'I know that.'

'Much worse than she was.'

'Where is all this going, Ellen?' he asked wearily.

'Have you seen Phil Dickie since that time?'

'No. Why should I have done? I don't even know if he's still alive.'

'Oh, he is. I saw him yesterday.'

'Really?' For the first time, his composure was slightly diminished. He and Grace exchanged looks.

'Phil Dickie had had a pretty rough time since he was airlifted from Beirut. He suffered from PTSD, apart from anything else.'

'I'm not surprised.'

'Became a bit reclusive, certainly didn't want to talk to the press about the events he'd witnessed.'

'Quite a common reaction. Those experiences take a lot of people that way. Whereas it only makes proper journalists hungry for more.'

I ignored his grandstanding. 'After he'd heard about Ingrid's death, Phil was prepared to talk to me about what he saw.'

'Oh?'

'Just before the car bomb was detonated, Ingrid was about to do a piece to camera. He was setting up to record it.'

'Not surprising. That was her job. And filming it was his job.'

'The piece to camera was about the hostage Paul McClennan. Ingrid had managed to make contact with one of his captors. She'd made arrangements, she'd bribed the right people, and was preparing to spring the hostage from the apartment in Southern Beirut where he was being held. She had asked Phil Dickie if he was prepared to take the risk of going with her to film the whole process. He'd agreed. It was the kind of coup he wanted to be part of.'

There was silence in the perfect sitting room. The way Grace Bellamy was looking at her husband told me that all of this was news to her too. Niall said nothing. I went on, 'Ingrid had put all the details of her mission, maps, passwords, names of contacts, into the leather satchel she always carried around with her.'

Still nothing from Niall. No reaction from the handsome, lived-in face.

'When the bomb exploded, Phil was thrown forward towards Ingrid. He saw she'd been hit in the forehead by shrapnel. Blood everywhere. He thought she'd been killed. But, just before he lost consciousness, Phil Dickie saw someone step forward and take the leather satchel from around her neck. He recognized you, Niall.'

'It isn't true!' This was from Grace. 'Tell her, darling! Tell her it's not true!'

Niall Connor smiled an infuriatingly calm smile. 'It doesn't make a lot of difference whether it is true or not. I rescued Paul McClennan. I sprang the hostage from where he was being held. That's the story that was reported in the world's press. And, of course, at the time there were people who said I couldn't have done it. Conspiracy theorists. There wasn't social media back then, thank God. But, even now, there are people out on Facebook and Twitter going on about Paul McClennan, saying that I didn't rescue him, that the Hezbollah handed him over for reasons of their own. It doesn't matter. The story's out there. No one's going to publish an alternative version. There's no one who can do it . . . particularly now the sainted Ingrid Richards is no longer with us.'

His smile had now turned triumphant. 'Well, Ellen, I don't think Grace and I need to entertain you and your conspiracy theory any longer. Unless there's some other wild accusation you want to offer us . . .?'

'There's more information I'd like to share with you,' I said.

'Oh? That's very generous.'

'I know, Niall, that you got in touch with Alexandra Richards after Ingrid's death.'

'Well, wasn't that nice of me? I wanted to commiserate with her. I am the girl's father, after all.'

'But why this sudden appearance of paternal feeling? You hadn't demonstrated much of it in her life up until then.'

'What are you saying, Ellen?' He sounded testy now. 'Could you get to the point?'

'All right. I think you cosied up to Alexandra because you

wanted her to hide the fact that you'd been to Ingrid's flat in Brunswick Square the evening before she died.'

He looked as if he was about to come up with some blustering denial but, after a slight head movement from Grace, he just said, 'And why would I do that?'

'Because you thought Alexandra would be so over the moon about your suddenly taking an interest in her, that she'd do as you asked.' A silence. 'Which is what happened. Though, by not revealing that you'd been to Ingrid's flat that evening, Alexandra very nearly got into trouble with the police.'

'Did she?' he asked drily.

'Did you know that she'd got a boyfriend?' I asked.

'No. I really know nothing about the girl. But isn't that heart-warming news?' he said snidely. 'It demonstrates the happy truth that there's someone for everyone, regardless of looks, doesn't it?'

'The boyfriend's name is Walt Rainbird.'

'Fascinating.'

'And, for reasons of his own, whose details I won't bother you with, he followed Alexandra from Hastings to Brunswick Square that evening and, parked in his car, he watched and made a note of everyone who went in and out of Ingrid's building.'

Niall Connor's face went suddenly pale. 'So he saw me?'

'He saw you go in. And he saw you come out.'

'Ah.'

'So, why did you go and see Ingrid Richards that evening, Niall?'

'Since you know about the memoir and since you've heard Phil Dickie's inaccurate account of events in Beirut in 1986, I think you ought to be able to answer that for yourself, Ellen.'

'All right.' He was still defiant, but cracks were beginning to appear in his carapace of confidence. I knew I could take my time. 'Then I would assume that you went to Brunswick Square to find out what Ingrid was planning to write in her memoir. Whether she was proposing to present an alternative version of the springing of Paul McClennan from captivity. In other words, to expose the fact that you'd only achieved the coup that transformed your professional life by stealing another journalist's research, by following the plans that another journalist had set up.'

'I see.'

I pressed on, 'And if Ingrid was planning that kind of exposé, I'm sure you were thinking of ways to stop her memoir from ever being published.'

'Oh, I see,' he said again. 'You're thinking that the fire which killed Ingrid was not an accident. That someone, knowing her habit of hoarding old newspapers, saw a way of removing her. That that someone, also knowing her drinking habits, doctored a bottle of Jameson's with crushed-up Zopiclone and—'

'How did you know about the Zopiclone?' Surely he wasn't going to fall for an old crime-fiction giveaway like that?

He wasn't. 'Alex told me about it,' he said. That was believable.

'So, Ellen . . .' He let the pause extend itself. 'You're accusing me of murdering Ingrid, aren't you?'

'I'd want to hear your version of events before I did that.'

'My version of events? My account of what happened that evening in Hove. "Hove, actually."' He was still determined to keep the tone light. 'Well, you and your unknown witness are correct. I did visit Ingrid Richards in her flat that evening. And yes, I did ask what she was proposing to put in her memoir about the springing of Paul McClennan in Beirut. And – surprise, surprise – she said she was going to offer an alternative view of history. I tried to dissuade her from doing so. She remained characteristically adamant that she would do what she wanted to do. Story of Ingrid Richards' life, really.

'I knew there was no point in arguing with her. And I comforted myself with the thought that she was really yesterday's news. Faces often seen on television tend to be very quickly forgotten, so I don't think a memoir of Ingrid Richards is going to sell in its millions. And, of course,' he grinned smugly, 'I got the story first. My book's been out there a long time and it's the banner headlines the public remember. No one ever reads the small print of a correction or an apology.' Another infuriating grin. 'So, are you still accusing me of murder, Ellen?'

'You haven't given me any reason not to,' I said doggedly.

'Ah, but there is a reason. A very compelling reason.'

'Oh?'

'As your mysterious witness parked in a car in Brunswick Square would be able to tell you, I left Ingrid's flat long before the fire started.'

'Yes. You did.' I turned to face Grace Bellamy. 'You didn't, though, did you? You got there much later.'

She turned paler than her husband had done.

'I referred Walt Rainbird to your website, so that he'd know what you looked like, and then he confirmed that you were the woman he saw enter Ingrid Richards' building at half-past eleven. You were carrying a bottle. A bottle of Jameson's, I would hazard a guess. Jameson's with a little extra ingredient. Walt saw you come out just before midnight, without the bottle.'

Niall Connor was looking with horror at Grace. He had felt confident in answering me, because he knew he had nothing to do with Ingrid Richards' death. But it had never occurred to him that his wife might have been involved.

For once, the perfect poise gave way. The finely modulated voice cracked as Grace Bellamy shouted, 'Can you blame me, Niall? All through our marriage, you kept talking about her. You kept comparing me to her. You kept implying that the sex you had with Ingrid was better than you ever had with me!'

'I didn't mean—'

'Oh, I don't think you even knew you were doing it. But she was there. Always there between us. After a time, I stopped worrying. Just as I stopped worrying about all your sordid little infidelities. Why should I be jealous of that line-up of tarts, because they all suffered from the same shortcoming as I did? They weren't Ingrid Bloody Richards!

'But I told myself, it's all right, I can cope with this. I'll come to terms with being second best. Lots of men fantasize about the lost love they had years before they ended up with reality, with their compromise wife. I could manage with that . . . until I found out that you were still seeing Ingrid!'

'But I wasn't still seeing—'

But Grace swept his question aside. 'No? You've just admitted you were in her flat that evening.'

'Yes, but that was the first time since—'

'I don't believe you. I know you were still seeing her, had been seeing her right through our marriage.'

'I hadn't. I just arranged to see her that evening to talk about the memoir. Like I said.'

'That's just not true, Niall!' There was a light of paranoia in the beautifully made-up eyes. 'I was certain you were up to something that evening, so I followed you down to Brighton. And, when we got Brunswick Square, I knew exactly where you were going.'

Of course. Grace had got Ingrid's contact details when she'd been trying to set up an interview with her. She'd also had some research done on the veteran correspondent's lifestyle. She knew about the piles of newspapers, the Gauloises, the Jameson's. Hence the bottle that Walt had seen her carrying into the building on Brunswick Square.

Both of them looked utterly defeated. Grace Bellamy was beginning to realize the enormity of what her jealousy had led her to. And Niall Connor was taking on board what his wife had done. Out of sheer jealousy.

TWENTY-FIVE

I was technically ahead of the police, in that I spoke to Ingrid Richards' murderer before they did. But they were way ahead of me in terms of building a case against Grace Bellamy. Of course, they had to have all their ducks in a row before they could bring charges against her.

After I left the Primrose Hill house, in a state of total exhaustion, I had been intending to ring Detective Sergeant Unwin and tell her where my research had led me. But, fortunately, when I got back to Chichester, I rang Alexandra Richards first.

Walt had persuaded her she had to come clean, tell Unwin and Gupta that she'd lied about staying in Brunswick Square all that evening. I don't know whether she told them that she'd lied because her absentee father had asked her to. And because she'd hoped that her obeying him would lead to a closer relationship between them.

Then Walt had volunteered to the police what he had seen from his car that evening in Hove. All the stuff he'd told me. Including the incriminating sight of Grace Bellamy entering the building.

Once they had a suspect, presumably the police could find forensic evidence of her presence in the burned-out flat. Or maybe she'd confessed to them, as she virtually had to me. I didn't know. The police tend not to share the details of their investigations with members of the public.

It struck me that they probably didn't contact Phil Dickie. Though he'd been a vital part of my researches, he wasn't relevant to theirs. While I believed Niall Connor had killed Ingrid Richards so that she would not publish her memoir and expose the treachery by which he had achieved the greatest scoop of his career, Phil Dickie was a vital part of my enquiries.

But what the police were investigating turned out to be no

more than a case of jealousy, a wife murdering her husband's lover. Commonplace stuff, really.

As a result, I never heard again from Detective Sergeants Unwin and Gupta, or anyone else involved in their investigation. Which was fine by me.

Back in Chichester, I continued running SpaceWoman, taking on new clients and, I hope, nurturing old ones.

I sent an invoice to Edward Finch. It was paid by return of post. A cheque, that increasingly rare object. No covering note. Thank God.

I don't know what's happened to him. I don't care. But I'm pretty sure, whatever he's doing, he still patronizes and takes advantage of the long-suffering Cara Reece. I'd be very surprised if he's allowed her to try on any of the new dresses which would have fitted Pauline. And me. Yuk. It makes me nauseous to think of it.

Minnie died at the end of the summer. And, predictably, I felt saddened. I even shed a tear when the care-home van delivered her collection of books about London which she'd left me in her will.

I haven't looked at them yet. Maybe I never will. I still don't feel comfortable about London.

Mary Griffin . . . Oh, Mary Griffin. I wish I could say I'd been like a fairy godmother and solved her problems. But life doesn't work like fairy stories. Yes, technically she's safe for the moment. She and Amy are in the house with their nice new furniture. I still drop in from time to time to see how they're doing. Amy's started school. Mary's made contact with some of the other mums outside the school gate. But she doesn't dare invite them to her house.

After what happened to Dodge, she still feels she's being watched. All the time. And the day will come when her husband Craig is released from prison.

Mary Griffin lives in permanent fear of that moment. And I wish I could take away that fear with some kind of magic wand. But I know I can't.

I've had virtually no contact from Alexandra Richards since that day when I came back from Primrose Hill. No reason why I should, I suppose, though I'm pretty sure Walt has discouraged her from getting in touch.

She did ring once, though, to say they were getting married. Of course, I offered lots of congratulations and said I was sure they'd be very happy together. Well, that's what you do, isn't it?

But I'm not sure marriage will bring long-term happiness to Alexandra Richards. I think Walt Rainbird, in his own, different, way, could prove to be quite as coercive a husband as Craig Griffin. Maybe I'm being cynical, though. And maybe Alexandra had been so starved of affection since birth that she'd welcome even the smothering kind.

Unsurprisingly, I haven't heard anything from Niall Connor. There was a big fuss in the press when Grace Bellamy came to trial and was convicted of murder. She was given a relatively light sentence in quite a relaxed prison. No doubt she's already writing a series of articles and a book about the experience.

On the domestic front, well . . . What I feared was inevitable has happened. Ben has once again dropped out of university. I've had very friendly conversations with someone who I think described himself as Ben's 'pastoral tutor'. He says he's sure Ben can restart his second year next year, but I wonder. It's happened once before. Ben could be in his thirties before he finishes his undergraduate course.

Right now, he needs to be at home with me, and I like that more than I should. He's got to face the real world at some point, and I know I should be encouraging him to get out and do something.

He claims he is doing things. He says he's working off his own bat on the 'Riq and Raq' animation, but again I wonder . . . Certainly spends a lot of time on his computer in his room but I'm not sure if he's achieving anything. I'd be delighted to be proved wrong, though. Some award for a Best Short Animation. I can dream. Mothers do about their children. Dream, and worry. Both go with the job description.

I'm afraid there's been no mention of Tracey since Ben's been back at home.

One good thing that's developed is that he's done more

work with Dodge, painting the furniture. It looks wonderful, they've done some brilliant stuff.

But even there I see problems ahead. True to his principles, Dodge doesn't want to make any money out of what they create. He wants to give it away to deserving causes. And Ben feels they should be more commercial, actually sell the stuff. It's certainly of a standard to compete in the market.

I know where Ben's coming from. It's not greed. It's guilt. He feels he should be making money, bringing in some income to defray the expenses of his living at home. It's not a problem for me from the financial point of view but I know, for Ben, it's a matter of pride.

Oh well, no doubt things will sort themselves out, one way or the other. And at least I know where my son is and what he's doing. Ben's so vulnerable and I love him so much. Too much, perhaps?

As for his sister . . . well, Jools and I have certainly had more contact since I went to Herne Hill. Still only brief phone calls, but more texts. All at a very superficial level. With me, as with Fleur, she'd gone back to the easier route of 'being someone else'. But I treasured that moment when she'd been 'herself' with me. And, knowing it was possible, I live in hope of it happening again some time. I'd have fallen apart long ago if I hadn't been an optimist at heart. Optimists frequently fly in the teeth of the evidence.

And, as to whether or not Jools had a hoarding problem . . . well, that was a subject that just didn't come up.

Then, of course, I had Fleur. The wonderful, infuriating, self-obsessed Fleur.

I remember, my first meeting with Alexandra, I felt a bond with her when she said her mother was famous. I think, if I was given the choice, I'd rather have spent time with Ingrid Richards than Fleur Bonnier any day. Unless, of course, I was her daughter.